Letters *from a* Self-Made Merchant *to his* Son

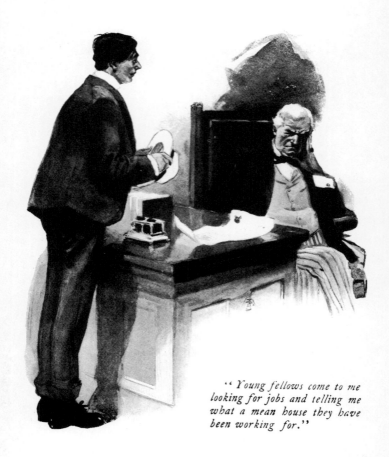

"*Young fellows come to me looking for jobs and telling me what a mean house they have been working for.*"

Letters from
A Self-Made Merchant
To His Son

Being the Letters written by John Graham,
Head of the House of Graham & Company,
Pork-Packers in Chicago, familiarly known
on 'Change as " Old Gorgon Graham," to
his Son, Pierrepont, facetiously known
to his intimates as " Piggy."

WITH A NEW INTRODUCTION BY

LAWRENCE GRAUMAN, JR.

AND

ROBERT S. FOGARTY

OUTERBRIDGE & DIENSTFREY

NEW YORK

DISTRIBUTED BY E. P. DUTTON & COMPANY

Library of Congress number 73-129971
Originally published in 1902
by Small, Maynard & Company (Incorporated)
This edition, with a new introduction, published
in the United States of America in 1970
Copyright © 1970 by Outerbridge & Dienstfrey.

Outerbridge & Dienstfrey
200 West 72 Street New York 10023

INTRODUCTION

Every few years the editors of the *Saturday Review,* the *American Scholar* and the *New York Times* ask a distinguished group of writers, critics and professors to list "favorite" or "forgotten" books that "changed America." Henry George's *Progress and Poverty* and Edward Bellamy's *Looking Backward* usually head the lists, but rarely mentioned is another work published during the same period, George Horace Lorimer's *Letters of a Self-Made Merchant to His Son*—a book that helped to create America and to sustain it.

Lorimer, "the Henry Ford of American literature," wrote no reformist tracts for his times, offered no visions of alternative cultures; he achieved his influence by "interpret[ing] America to itself" ("always readably, but constructively") in the pages of the *Saturday Evening Post,* and by composing several serial accounts of business adventure and practical wisdom, the first of which, *Letters of a Self-Made Merchant to His Son,* enjoyed a reception exceptional even by the standards of his own magazine.

Just as Benjamin Franklin's *The Way to Wealth* serves to introduce and to complement Franklin's distinguished public career, Lorimer's *Letters* complements his forty-year career as edi-

INTRODUCTION

tor of the *Saturday Evening Post*. For from 1899
to 1936 Lorimer was responsible for the growth
and management of the magazine which, in the
judgment of the *New York Times,* "probably
had more influence on the cultural life of America" than any other periodical in our history. As
his publisher Cyrus H. K. Curtis put it: "Lorimer
is the *Post* and the *Post* is Lorimer." And the
Post spoke for the silent majority long before
that constituency knew itself and knew it was
cherished, and Lorimer spoke most directly *to* it
in the anonymously printed twenty-part series of
letters than ran from late 1901 to early 1902.
Subsequently the *Letters* appeared as a book,
published by Small, Maynard and Company of
Boston, sold over 300,000 copies, was simulta-
neously a best seller in the United States, England and Germany, was translated into more
than 12 languages, and was reprinted as inspira-
tional literature by major corporations like the
Eastman Kodak Company. It has been estimated
that this book was translated into more languages
and was more generally circulated throughout
the world than any other book by an American
author since *Uncle Tom's Cabin.*

Lorimer's how-to-succeed tract was not unre-
lated to his own advancement. He was born in
1867 in Louisville, Kentucky, to the Reverend
George Lorimer, pastor of the large though debt-

ridden Walnut Street Baptist Church. After putting the church on its feet, the Reverend Lorimer moved to churches in Albany, New York, to the famous Tremont Temple in Boston, and then, in 1879, to the First Baptist Church of Chicago. Lorimer, Sr., was a vibrant, aggressive preacher who took old properties and gave them new life; in 1899 his son did the same thing for the bankrupt *Post*.

By 1888, however, young Lorimer had progressed only as far as Yale University where, during his one year there, a chance meeting with Philip D. Armour (one of his father's parishioners at the fashionable Immanuel Baptist Church in Chicago) changed the course of his career. The meat-packing magnate told the undergraduate to "give up that nonsense" and come to work for Armour and Company. According· to one account, Armour promised: "I'll make you a millionaire." Lorimer left Yale and within five years was head of the canning department.

But canning, at least of meat, was too confining for Lorimer, and he returned to school, this time to Colby College in Maine, to develop some practical writing skills for his new profession, journalism. During the late 1890s he worked on several Boston papers until he moved to Philadelphia and a job as "literary editor" with Cyrus Curtis' *Saturday Evening Post*. Curtis had purchased the bankrupt *Post* in 1897 and hoped to turn it into the male equivalent of the *Ladies Home Journal,* which was a proven success under the direction of the brilliant and self-assertive Edward Bok. In 1899 the editorship of the *Post* fell vacant for a few months and Lorimer was appointed interim managing editor. While Curtis was in Europe trying to arrange a meeting with a distinguished editor named Arthur Sherburne Hardy, Lorimer moved quickly to make the magazine a success. In the words of Old Gorgon Graham, the self-made merchant of the letters to come, he seized the main chance.

Lorimer wanted to make the *Post* a national magazine with emphasis on both America's past achievements and its future social and commercial promise. It was, according to the historian of the *Post,* John Tebbel, to be "a magazine without class, clique or sectional editing, but intended for every adult in America's seventy-five million population." Although Lorimer was to issue periodic reaffirmations of this inclusive editorial policy, he began almost immediately to produce a magazine with a dominant appeal to young, middle-class, professionally ambitious White Anglo-Saxon Protestant men. And although he aimed to entertain first, to challenge occasionally, and to continue selling the magazine for five cents a copy ("It promises twice as much as any other magazine, and it will try to give twice as much as it promises"), Lorimer believed that he must also develop a distinctive editorial image for the *Post*, a character of its own. He discovered the source of this character in the themes of business success, "public affairs" and romantic fiction— themes which could be overlapped and co-mingled so as to reveal the romance and adventure of commercial enterprise, or the politics of professional ambition, and could yield opportunities for humor and for the depiction of "personalities."

So Lorimer broadened the base of the *Post's* readership, intensified its appeal to a more or less special audience, and began to soothe a public grown weary of radicalism, war, social discord, and weary even of the rhetoric of uplift. He captured a reflection of the surface of American life, and although he published some powerful fiction (by Stephen Crane, Bret Harte, Jack London and Frank Norris) and some valuable muckraking (by David Graham Phillips) the reflection caught by the *Post* was a distorted one which slighted the depredations of big business, glorified imperialist impulses, intensified nativism, romanticised and patronized Negro life, and subordinated most literature within the dimensions of formula.

INTRODUCTION

When Curtis purchased the *Saturday Evening Post* its circulation was at 2,000, but by 1902 it was 350,000, by 1908 a million (which figure Lorimer immediately emblazoned on the cover), by 1919 two million, and at the time of Lorimer's retirement in 1936 three million. The first great leap in circulation came when Lorimer began to run the *Letters of a Self-Made Merchant to His Son* in the autumn of 1901, and his decision to undertake this series was a result of his persistent effort to refine the distinctive appeal of the *Post*.

Lorimer regarded business as a wonderful and romantic adventure. He had encouraged this kind of depiction in articles by and about businessmen, but he determined that it could also be rendered in fiction. Harold Frederic's "The Market Place," which John Tebbel has called the first successful attempt to write a business story, had appeared in the *Post* the month Lorimer was made editor, but Frederic died before the story was published, and none of the other writers Lorimer approached were willing to experiment in this new mode. His attempts to persuade fiction writers to see that every business day was full of comedy, tragedy, farce and romance ("the struggle for existence is the loaf, love or sex is the frosting on the cake") finally convinced Lorimer that he himself was best qualified to take on the commission. He quietly began to write a series of five or six pieces.

The public response was so overwhelmingly favorable that Lorimer continued the series through twenty letters, which extended publication into 1902. Before the end of 1901 he had received 5,000 letters of approval, encouragement and suggestion from readers of the *Post*. Newspapers in Boston quickly cadged the format and by 1903 were running series with titles like: "Letters from a Self-Made Chorus Girl to Her Hand-Made Mother" and "Letters from a Custom-Made Son to His Ready-Made Father." Thus through the *Letters* Lorimer spoke to and for a confident, productive mercantile age which was ready to revel in the adventure of business. Or, as Frank Luther Mott, the great chronicler of American journalism, has put it: "the *Post* made its first spectacular success by a whole-hearted devotion to material prosperity, and by directing young men to that goal."

Moreover, American society at the turn of the century confronted its mythmakers with expectations that required for their fulfillment a further refinement and elaboration of the American Dream. Benjamin Franklin's virtuous suggestions and Andrew Carnegie's admonition to be "king in your dreams" simply did not meet the needs of the emerging culture of 20th century finance capitalism. Just as the mass circulation *Post* and *Ladies Home Journal* eclipsed the lordly *Atlantic* and the frosty *Nation*—only to be eclipsed in our time by *Playboy* and *Time*—so did Lorimer's *Letters* offer an experience which wasn't available in the stories of Horatio Alger and Orson Sweet Marden. There is in the *Letters* none of the sentiment and chance, none of that high moral tone which characterized Alger's *Brave and Bold* or Marden's *Pushing to the Front; or Success Under Difficulties (A Book of Inspiration and Encouragement to All Who Are Struggling for Self-Elevation Along the Paths of Knowledge and of Duty)*. There is a tacit recognition in these letters that the histrionics and the uplift of Alger's heroes were as obsolete as Carnegie's steel company—which became U.S. Steel in 1901.

Even as the *Letters* provides a more relevant and durable moral resource for the ambitious young businessmen who had outgrown uplift, it also anticipates those conditions of industry that would finally determine success. Between 1899 and 1901 (the years of Lorimer's ascendency) the modern corporation became increasingly visible as consolidations, mergers and trust formations transformed the face of American business. U.S.

INTRODUCTION

Steel became the first billion dollar corporation and the *Saturday Evening Post* its prophet. A typical expression of Lorimer's attitude can be found in a *Post* editorial following the 1901 assassination of McKinley and the elevation of Theodore Roosevelt to the presidency:

> We, who give such chances of success to all so that it is possible for a young man to go as a laborer into the steel business and before he has reached his mature prime become, through his own industry and talent, the president of a vast steel association—we who make this possible as no country has ever made it possible have been stabbed in the back by anarchy.

Clearly anarchy was not the way to wealth, but Alger's formula of virtue and good fortune was not very helpful either. In his *Letters*, Lorimer redefines the values of the American Dream—hard work, perseverance, self-reliance, puritanism, the missionary spirit, the abstract rule of law—by the hard and cunning code of his time, and he offers his readers a current version of the process of Americanization (or socialization, as school psychologists now call it) which they could accept as both necessary and reasonable. Although Old Gorgon Graham is speaking to his son and heir apparent, the readers of the *Post* could still regard the correspondence as a viable model of this process.

Lorimer's book, then, is full of a cheerful cynicism, a genial contempt, which both mirrors and contradicts the vision of an open, democratic society. Its version of the rags-to-riches theme, for example, was as illusive in reality as it was beguiling in theory: most of the captains of industry, as William Miller has demonstrated, came from settled, professional families who were third or fourth generation Americans. In fact, a large percentage of the 19th century business leaders had been—like Lorimer—aided by their father's connections.

In other words, George Horace Lorimer contributed as much as anyone toward the transformation of the American Dream into the American Myth.

It would be irrelevant if not futile to read this "novel" with the expectations stimulated by modern literary criticism. Although there is much humor here, there is no irony. Although there is contradiction, there is no ambiguity. Although there is much moralizing, there is no moral tension. "Plot development," such as it is, is crude and static, and although Lorimer generally finds the epistolary format quite serviceable, he doesn't hesitate to employ *non-sequiturs* or to force the introduction of helpful characters. While one may assume that the point of view is not identical with Lorimer's own, it is close enough, and otherwise so obvious, as to require little discussion. (During serial publication a number of readers wrote Lorimer suggesting that he print the letters of the son, but, once one has completed the book, Pierrepont's representations and his complete capitulation are so evident that this is unnecessary—not to say unimaginable.) The book depends for its effect almost entirely upon a resourceful and accurate use of language, on Lorimer's ear for vernacular and for the rhythms of spoken speech, and this dependence is worth noting.

Although Lorimer draws upon an impressively fertile fund of figurative expression, including aphorisms, epigrams, homilies, inverted proverbs and home-grown similes, contemporary readers may find the pattern of repetition tedious. Of course the letters were originally published serially in the *Post,* and so it is doubtful that Lorimer worried much about this limitation of his literary formula. Moreover, he could overcome mere repetition through the clever if not subtle deployment of all those metaphors and similes in which he reinforces the form by giving substantive examples of the moral or economic purpose. (Thus: "The boy who does anything just because the other fellows do it is apt to scratch a poor

INTRODUCTION

man's back all his life. He's the chap that's buying wheat at ninety-seven cents the day before
the market breaks. They call him 'the country'
in the market reports, but the city's full of him."
Or "A man can't have his head pumped out like
a vacuum pan, or stuffed full of odds and ends
like a bologna sausage, and do his work right.")
Actually this device represents Lorimer's only
concession to "literary" calculation; for the most
part he relies on a remarkable ability to repro-
duce the language of a particular region and
class, and on an accurate memory of his models.

The style of the *Letters* derives from several
well-established popular traditions, not the least
of which is the hortatorical, anecdotal, exemplary
mode of autobiography prepared for by John
Bunyan and Cotton Mather, consummated by
Benjamin Franklin, and imitated by Andrew
Carnegie, Booker T. Washington and many
others.* (Lorimer, of course, did not share Franklin's concern for the proper "mask," an aware-
ness of a reconstructed self appropriate to the
public circumstance. He was in this respect a
single-minded man.) And this work is also a

---

*The analogy between the careers of Lorimer and
Benjamin Franklin is quite interesting, and in the
1930s was carried to some illogical extremes by a
hostile though competent critic named Benjamin Stol-
berg (writing in the *Outlook and Independent* magazine).

INTRODUCTION

product of the oral tradition of American folk humor, a tradition preserved in the "local color" literature of the 19th century, and represented by such disparate writers as Finley Peter Dunne, Thomas Bangs Thorpe, Max Adler and, of course, Mark Twain.

Lorimer's distinctive achievement in the *Letters* is the fusion of these cultural styles of 18th and 19th century America into the language of the "new man" of the early 20th century. What is interesting in this book is what John Graham says (or doesn't), and how he says it, rather than what he does or thinks about or what others think of him. The Old Gorgon tells us not only everything his creator would like us to know about him —how he exalts his mid-Western origins, how he scorns academic education and patrician advantage, his primal faith in willful self-assertion, his pride in independence and sheer competence, his transcendent respect for buck success—but also tells us everything we need to know about him— his contempt for art and literature, his nativist and anti-immigration assumptions (suggested by his patronizing defense of Milligan), his stereotypical dismissal of "niggers," his narrow, unambiguous estimate of human potential and the possibilities of pleasure. The language which expresses these assumptions and values is appropriate to the circumstances of a self-made and

unregulated meat packing magnate, but beneath
this there is an underlying pattern of linguistic
evidence which reveals more about the writer
than he perhaps intended us to know. Even when
Lorimer throws in a stock phrase from the speech
of his old friend, P. D. Armour (who was the
inspiration for John Graham, though not really
the "model," as some have assumed), a reflexive
expression like "I simply mention this in passing"—nostalgically recalled for flavor—tells us a
good deal about the carrot-and-stick technique of
Piggy's socialization.

Finally, this is the language of a particular
time and place: Chicago at the turn of the century. Shortly after the *Letters* was published,
Lorimer's editor asked William Allen White to
write something about the book that could be
used as advertising copy. White wrote back:

> The best thing about George Horace Lori-
> mer's *Letters* . . . is that they tell the truth
> about Chicago so unconsciously. Lorimer
> . . . has created a paper man as vital as any
> of the men made by American story writers.
> John Graham is strong, hard-working,
> broad-gauged after the Western fashion,
> mean to his enemies, provincial, country-
> bred, city-made, an automatic philanthro-
> pist and what the country papers call "a
> kind father, a loyal husband, a generous
> friend and a good citizen." Graham has

more philosophy than the Shepherd of Arden, but it is the philosophy of business; cynical as the cold south wind. But the marvel of the whole book, John Graham, Pierrepont, his "Ma," Helen Heath, and all of the simple dramatis personae, is the way it reproduces and reflects Chicago. In no other book is the dirt and riches and unformed mass of the town more vividly yet unconsciously set down than in these *Letters*. The book is Chicago boiled to an essence. The barbaric yawp of protest, and the careless whoop of approval that Chicago voices where she pleases, are in the book. If a statue typical of Chicago were to be made it should represent John Graham writing to his son, "Repartee makes lively reading but business dull. What the house needs is more orders."

White is largely right, as far as he goes. Had he written his endorsement only a couple of years later he might have gone further and suggested that the *rest* of the "truth about Chicago" was to be found in a new book by Upton Sinclair called *The Jungle*.* Although they lived only a few

*Sinclair was one of the most extreme critics of the *Saturday Evening Post*, of which he wrote, in *Money Writes!,* that its "stuff is as standardized as soda crackers: originality is taboo, new ideas are treason, social sympathy is a crime, and the one virtue of man is to produce larger and larger quantities of material things." And then he printed George Sterling's poem,

miles apart, and worked in the same place, John Graham and Sinclair's Jurgis Antanas could no more have shared the experience or agreed on the meaning of Chicago than, in a later day, could Julius and Abbie Hoffman have shared an understanding of that same city.

"The Black Hound Bays." Here are a few lines from that ballad:

> The Lords of the Nation go hunting with their dogs;
> Some have the hearts of tigers, and some the hearts of hogs.
> On the path of the quarry the yapping mongrels pour,
> And the keenest of the pack is the great dog Lorrimor.
>
> "Woo, hoo, hoo, hoo! O Lords, spare not the spur!
> Give me the white doe Freedom, that I flesh my fangs in her!
> I ha' hate for all wild hearts!" bays the dog Lorrimor . . . .
>
> Oh, lavish is his tongue for the feet of all his Lords!
> And hoarse is his throat if a foot go near their hoards.
> Sharp are his teeth and savage is his heart,
> When he lifts up his voice to drown the song of Art.
> . . . . . .
>
> If the young folk build an altar to their vision of the New,
> Be sure the great dog Lorrimor shall lift a leg thereto.

INTRODUCTION

The present generation of middle-aged Americans includes probably the last majority of people in this country to have had direct, first-hand experience of paternal attitudes derived from John Graham's philosophy. It is doubtful that many parents could still accept such deceptively simple wisdom, much less pass it on in good conscience to their children. For that matter it is doubtful that we will see any more books composed of letters written by a father to his son. (If indeed American fathers and their sons even write to each other any longer.) The very form of this book is obsolete, since it presupposes an entirely different notion of social and family stability than that which has obtained for at least a generation.

But this is not to say that a book like *Letters of a Self-Made Merchant to His Son* does not bear upon the present age. It bears so hard that some will call it oppressive. For George Horace Lorimer was one of those who invented this country, its culture and its values. He and his white Anglo-Saxon Protestant contemporaries were those who articulated and analyzed American ideas, who shaped our institutions, and who embodied what we were or hoped to be. They achieved dominance as initiators and entrepreneurs. Then their sons drew our institutions around themselves, moved to the suburbs, and became organization men. And now their grandsons are saying that they must build a "counter culture." If they are serious they might begin by reading Lorimer, for his is the culture they will have to counter.

LAWRENCE GRAUMAN, JR.
Editor, The Antioch Review
ROBERT S. FOGARTY
Antioch College

CONTENTS

XXVii

CONTENTS

CONTENTS

CONTENTS

CONTENTS

ILLUSTRATIONS

By F. R. GRUGER *and* B. MARTIN JUSTICE

ILLUSTRATIONS

No. 1

FROM John Graham, at the Union Stock Yards in Chicago, to his son, Pierrepont, at Harvard University, Cambridge, Mass. Mr. Pierrepont has just been settled by his mother as a member, in good and regular standing, of the Freshman class.

LETTERS *from a* SELF-MADE MERCHANT *to his* SON

CHICAGO, October 1, 189—

Dear Pierrepont: Your Ma got back safe this morning and she wants me to be sure to tell you not to over-study, and I want to tell you to be sure not to under-study. What we're really sending you to Harvard for is to get a little of the education that's so good and plenty there. When it's passed around you don't want to be bashful, but reach right out and take a big helping every time, for I want you to get your share. You'll find that education's about the only thing lying around loose in this world, and that it's about the only thing a fellow can have as much of as he's willing to haul away. Everything else is screwed down tight and the screw-driver lost.

I didn't have your advantages when I was a boy, and you can't have mine. Some men learn the value of money by not having any and starting out to pry a few dollars loose from the odd millions that are lying around; and some learn it by having fifty thousand or so left to them and starting out to spend it as if it were fifty thousand a year. Some men learn the value of truth by having to do business with liars; and some by going to Sunday School. Some men learn the cussedness of whiskey by having a drunken father; and some by having a good mother. Some men get an education from other men and newspapers and public libraries; and some get it from professors and parchments—it doesn't make any special difference how you get a half-nelson on the right thing, just so you get it and freeze on to it. The package doesn't count after the eye's been attracted by it, and in the end it finds its way to the ash heap. It's the quality of the goods inside which tells, when they once get into the kitchen and up to the cook.

2

You can cure a ham in dry salt and you can cure it in sweet pickle, and when you're through you've got pretty good eating either way, provided you started in with a sound ham. If you didn't, it doesn't make any special difference how you cured it—the ham-tryer's going to strike the sour spot around the bone. And it doesn't make any difference how much sugar and fancy pickle you soak into a fellow, he's no good unless he's sound and sweet at the core.

The first thing that any education ought to give a man is character, and the second thing is education. That is where I'm a little skittish about this college business. I'm not starting in to preach to you, because I know a young fellow with the right sort of stuff in him preaches to himself harder than any one else can, and that he's mighty often switched off the right path by having it pointed out to him in the wrong way.

I remember when I was a boy, and I wasn't a very bad boy, as boys go, old Doc

3

Hoover got a notion in his head that I ought to join the church, and he scared me out of it for five years by asking me right out loud in Sunday School if I didn't want to be saved, and then laying for me after the service and praying with me. Of course I wanted to be saved, but I didn't want to be saved quite so publicly.

When a boy's had a good mother he's got a good conscience, and when he's got a good conscience he don't need to have right and wrong labeled for him. Now that your Ma's left and the apron strings are cut, you're naturally running up against a new sensation every minute, but if you'll simply use a little conscience as a tryer, and probe into a thing which looks sweet and sound on the skin, to see if you can't fetch up a sour smell from around the bone, you'll be all right.

I'm anxious that you should be a good scholar, but I'm more anxious that you should be a good clean man. And if you

4

" *Old Doc Hoover asked me right out in Sunday School if I didn't want to be saved.*"

graduate with a sound conscience, I shan't care so much if there are a few holes in your Latin. There are two parts of a college education—the part that you get in the schoolroom from the professors, and the part that you get outside of it from the boys. That's the really important part. For the first can only make you a scholar, while the second can make you a man.

Education's a good deal like eating—a fellow can't always tell which particular thing did him good, but he can usually tell which one did him harm. After a square meal of roast beef and vegetables, and mince pie and watermelon, you can't say just which ingredient is going into muscle, but you don't have to be very bright to figure out which one started the demand for pain-killer in your insides, or to guess, next morning, which one made you believe in a personal devil the night before. And so, while a fellow can't figure out to an ounce whether it's Latin or algebra or history or what among the solids that is building him up in this place or that, he can go right along feeding them in and betting that they're not the things that turn his tongue fuzzy. It's down among the sweets, among his amusements and recreations, that he's going to find his stomach-ache, and it's there that he wants to go slow and to pick and choose.

It's not the first half, but the second half of a college education which merchants mean when they ask if a college education pays. It's the Willie and the Bertie boys; the chocolate eclair and tutti-frutti boys; the la-de-dah and the baa-baa-billy-goat boys; the high cock-a-lo-rum and the cock-a-doodle-do boys; the Bah Jove!, hair-parted - in - the - middle, cigaroot - smoking, Champagne-Charlie, up-all-night-and-in-all-day boys that make 'em doubt the cash value of the college output, and overlook the roast-beef and blood-gravy boys, the shirt-sleeves and high-water-pants boys, who take their college education and make some fellow's business hum with it.

Does a College education pay? Does it pay to feed in pork trimmings at five cents a pound at the hopper and draw out nice, cunning, little "country" sausages at twenty cents a pound at the other end? Does it pay to take a steer that's been running loose on the range and living on cactus and petrified wood till he's just a bunch of barb-wire and sole-leather, and feed him corn till he's just a solid hunk of porterhouse steak and oleo oil?

You bet it pays. Anything that trains a boy to think and to think quick pays; anything that teaches a boy to get the answer before the other fellow gets through biting the pencil, pays.

College doesn't make fools; it develops them. It doesn't make bright men; it develops them. A fool will turn out a fool, whether he goes to college or not, though he'll probably turn out a different sort of a

7

fool. And a good, strong boy will turn out a bright, strong man whether he's worn smooth in the grab-what-you-want-and-eat-standing - with - one - eye - skinned - for-the-dog school of the streets and stores, or polished up and slicked down in the give-your - order - to - the - waiter - and - get - a-sixteen - course - dinner school of the professors. But while the lack of a college education can't keep No. 1 down, having it boosts No. 2 up.

It's simply the difference between jump in, rough-and-tumble, kick-with-the-heels-and-butt-with-the-head nigger fighting, and this grin-and-look-pleasant, dodge-and-save-your - wind - till - you - see - a - chance - to-land-on-the-solar-plexus style of the trained athlete. Both styles win fights, but the fellow with a little science is the better man, providing he's kept his muscle hard. If he hasn't, he's in a bad way, for his fancy sparring is just going to aggravate the other fellow so that he'll eat him up.

8

Of course, some men are like pigs, the more you educate them, the more amusing little cusses they become, and the funnier capers they cut when they show off their tricks. Naturally, the place to send a boy of that breed is to the circus, not to college.

Speaking of educated pigs, naturally calls to mind the case of old man Whitaker and his son, Stanley. I used to know the old man mighty well ten years ago. He was one of those men whom business narrows, instead of broadens. Didn't get any special fun out of his work, but kept right along at it because he didn't know anything else. Told me he'd had to root for a living all his life and that he proposed to have Stan's brought to him in a pail. Sent him to private schools and dancing schools and colleges and universities, and then shipped him to Oxford to soak in a little "atmosphere," as he put it. I never could quite lay hold of that atmosphere dodge by the tail, but so far as I could make out, the idea was

9

that there was something in the air of the Oxford ham-house that gave a fellow an extra fancy smoke.

Well, about the time Stan was through, the undertaker called by for the old man, and when his assets were boiled down and the water drawn off, there wasn't enough left to furnish Stan with a really nourishing meal. I had a talk with Stan about what he was going to do, but some ways he didn't strike me as having the making of a good private of industry, let alone a captain, so I started in to get him a job that would suit his talents. Got him in a bank, but while he knew more about the history of banking than the president, and more about political economy than the board of directors, he couldn't learn the difference between a fiver that the Government turned out and one that was run off on a hand press in a Halsted Street basement. Got him a job on a paper, but while he knew six different languages and all the facts about

the Arctic regions, and the history of dancing from the days of Old Adam down to
those of Old Nick, he couldn't write up a
satisfactory account of the Ice-Men's Ball.
Could prove that two and two made four
by trigonometry and geometry, but couldn't
learn to keep books; was thick as thieves
with all the high-toned poets, but couldn't
write a good, snappy, merchantable street-
car ad.; knew a thousand diseases that
would take a man off before he could blink,
but couldn't sell a thousand-dollar tontine
policy; knew the lives of our Presidents as
well as if he'd been raised with them, but
couldn't place a set of the Library of the
Fathers of the Republic, though they were
offered on little easy payments that made
them come as easy as borrowing them from
a friend. Finally I hit on what seemed to
be just the right thing. I figured out that
any fellow who had such a heavy stock of
information on hand, ought to be able to job
it out to good advantage, and so I got him

a place teaching. But it seemed that he'd learned so much about the best way of teaching boys, that he told his principal right on the jump that he was doing it all wrong, and that made him sore; and he knew so much about the dead languages, which was what he was hired to teach, that he forgot he was handling live boys, and as he couldn't tell it all to them in the regular time, he kept them after hours, and that made them sore and put Stan out of a job again. The last I heard of him he was writing articles on Why Young Men Fail, and making a success of it, because failing was the one subject on which he was practical.

I simply mention Stan in passing as an example of the fact that it isn't so much knowing a whole lot, as knowing a little and how to use it that counts.

Your affectionate father,
JOHN GRAHAM.

No. 2

FROM John Graham, at the Union Stock Yards in Chicago, to his son, Pierrepont, at Harvard University. Mr. Pierrepont's expense account has just passed under his father's eye, and has furnished him with a text for some plain particularities.

II

Dear Pierrepont: The cashier has just handed me your expense account for the month, and it fairly makes a fellow hump-shouldered to look it over. When I told you that I wished you to get a liberal education, I didn't mean that I wanted to buy Cambridge. Of course the bills won't break me, but they will break you unless you are very, very careful.

I have noticed for the last two years that your accounts have been growing heavier every month, but I haven't seen any signs of your taking honors to justify the increased operating expenses; and that is bad business—a good deal like feeding his weight in corn to a scalawag steer that won't fat up.

I haven't said anything about this before, as I trusted a good deal to your native common-sense to keep you from making a fool

15

of yourself in the way that some of these young fellows who haven't had to work for it do. But because I have sat tight, I don't want you to get it into your head that the old man's rich, and that he can stand it, because he won't stand it after you leave college. The sooner you adjust your spending to what your earning capacity will be, the easier they will find it to live together.

The only sure way that a man can get rich quick is to have it given to him or to inherit it. You are not going to get rich that way—at least, not until after you have proved your ability to hold a pretty important position with the firm; and, of course, there is just one place from which a man can start for that position with Graham & Co. It doesn't make any difference whether he is the son of the old man or of the cellar boss—that place is the bottom. And the bottom in the office end of this business is a seat at the mailing-desk, with eight dollars every Saturday night.

I can't hand out any ready-made success to you. It would do you no good, and it would do the house harm. There is plenty of room at the top here, but there is no elevator in the building. Starting, as you do, with a good education, you should be able to climb quicker than the fellow who hasn't got it; but there's going to be a time when you begin at the factory when you won't be able to lick stamps so fast as the other boys at the desk. Yet the man who hasn't licked stamps isn't fit to write letters. Naturally, that is the time when knowing whether the pie comes before the ice-cream, and how to run an automobile isn't going to be of any real use to you.

I simply mention these things because I am afraid your ideas as to the basis on which you are coming with the house have swelled up a little in the East. I can give you a start, but after that you will have to dynamite your way to the front by yourself. It is all with the man. If you gave some

17

fellows a talent wrapped in a napkin to start with in business, they would swap the talent for a gold brick and lose the napkin; and there are others that you could start out with just a napkin, who would set up with it in the dry-goods business in a small way, and then coax the other fellow's talent into it.

I have pride enough to believe that you have the right sort of stuff in you, but I want to see some of it come out. You will never make a good merchant of yourself by reversing the order in which the Lord decreed that we should proceed—learning the spending before the earning end of business. Pay day is always a month off for the spendthrift, and he is never able to realize more than sixty cents on any dollar that comes to him. But a dollar is worth one hundred and six cents to a good business man, and he never spends the dollar. It's the man who keeps saving up and expenses down that buys an interest in the concern. That

18

is where you are going to find yourself weak if your expense accounts don't lie; and they generally don't lie in that particular way, though Baron Munchausen was the first traveling man, and my drummers' bills still show his influence.

I know that when a lot of young men get off by themselves, some of them think that recklessness with money brands them as good fellows, and that carefulness is meanness. That is the one end of a college education which is pure cussedness; and that is the one thing which makes nine business men out of ten hesitate to send their boys off to school. But on the other hand, that is the spot where a young man has the chance to show that he is not a lightweight. I know that a good many people say I am a pretty close proposition; that I make every hog which goes through my packing-house give up more lard than the Lord gave him gross weight; that I have improved on Nature to the extent of getting four hams out of an animal which began life with two; but you have lived with me long enough to know that my hand is usually in my pocket at the right time.

Now I want to say right here that the meanest man alive is the one who is generous with money that he has not had to sweat for, and that the boy who is a good fellow at some one else's expense would not work up into first-class fertilizer. That same ambition to be known as a good fellow has crowded my office with second-rate clerks, and they always will be second-rate clerks. If you have it, hold it down until you have worked for a year. Then, if your ambition runs to hunching up all week over a desk, to earn eight dollars to blow on a few rounds of drinks for the boys on Saturday night, there is no objection to your gratifying it; for I will know that the Lord didn't intend you to be your own boss.

You know how I began—I was started off

"*I have seen hundreds of boys go to Europe who didn't bring back a great deal except a few trunks of badly fitting clothes.*"

with a kick, but that proved a kick up, and in the end every one since has lifted me a little bit higher. I got two dollars a week, and slept under the counter, and you can bet I knew just how many pennies there were in each of those dollars, and how hard the floor was. That is what you have got to learn.

I remember when I was on the Lakes, our schooner was passing out through the draw at Buffalo when I saw little Bill Riggs, the butcher, standing up above me on the end of the bridge with a big roast of beef in his basket. They were a little short in the galley on that trip, so I called up to Bill and he threw the roast down to me. I asked him how much, and he yelled back, " about a dollar." That was mighty good beef, and when we struck Buffalo again on the return trip, I thought I would like a little more of it. So I went up to Bill's shop and asked him for a piece of the same. But this time he gave me a little roast, not near so big as

2I

the other, and it was pretty tough and stringy. But when I asked him how much, he answered " about a dollar." He simply didn't have any sense of values, and that's the business man's sixth sense. Bill has always been a big, healthy, hard-working man, but to-day he is very, very poor.

The Bills ain't all in the butcher business. I've got some of them right now in my office, but they will never climb over the railing that separates the clerks from the executives. Yet if they would put in half the time thinking for the house that they give up to hatching out reasons why they ought to be allowed to overdraw their salary accounts, I couldn't keep them out of our private offices with a pole-ax, and I wouldn't want to; for they could double their salaries and my profits in a year. But I always lay it down as a safe proposition that the fellow who has to break open the baby's bank toward the last of the week for car-fare isn't going to be any Russell Sage when it comes

to trading with the old man's money. He'd
punch my bank account as full of holes as a
carload of wild Texans would a fool stock-
man that they'd got in a corner.

Now I know you'll say that I don't understand how it is; that you've got to do as
the other fellows do; and that things have
changed since I was a boy. There's nothing
in it. Adam invented all the different ways
in which a young man can make a fool of
himself, and the college yell at the end of
them is just a frill that doesn't change es-
sentials. The boy who does anything just
because the other fellows do it is apt to
scratch a poor man's back all his life. He's
the chap that's buying wheat at ninety-
seven cents the day before the market
breaks. They call him "the country" in
the market reports, but the city's full of
him. It's the fellow who has the spunk to
think and act for himself, and sells short
when prices hit the high C and the house is
standing on its hind legs yelling for more,

that sits in the directors' meetings when he gets on toward forty.

We've got an old steer out at the packing-house that stands around at the foot of the runway leading up to the killing pens, looking for all the world like one of the village fathers sitting on the cracker box before the grocery—sort of sad-eyed, dreamy old cuss —always has two or three straws from his cud sticking out of the corner of his mouth. You never saw a steer that looked as if he took less interest in things. But by and by the boys drive a bunch of steers toward him, or cows maybe, if we're canning, and then you'll see Old Abe move off up that runway, sort of beckoning the bunch after him with that wicked old stump of a tail of his, as if there was something mighty interesting to steers at the top, and something that every Texan and Colorado, raw from the prairies, ought to have a look at to put a metropolitan finish on him. Those steers just naturally follow along on up that runway and

24

into the killing pens. But just as they get to the top, Old Abe, someways, gets lost in the crowd, and he isn't among those present when the gates are closed and the real trouble begins for his new friends.

I never saw a dozen boys together that there wasn't an Old Abe among them. If you find your crowd following him, keep away from it. There are times when it's safest to be lonesome. Use a little common-sense, caution and conscience. You can stock a store with those three commodities, when you get enough of them. But you've got to begin getting them young. They ain't catching after you toughen up a bit.

You needn't write me if you feel your-self getting them. The symptoms will show in your expense account. Good-by; life's too short to write letters and New York's calling me on the wire.

Your affectionate father,
JOHN GRAHAM.

No. 3

FROM John Graham, at the Union Stock Yards in Chicago, to his son, Pierrepont, at Harvard University. Mr. Pierrepont finds Cambridge to his liking, and has suggested that he take a post-graduate course to fill up some gaps which he has found in his education.

III

Dear Pierrepont: No, I can't say that I think anything of your post-graduate course idea. You're not going to be a poet or a professor, but a packer, and the place to take a post-graduate course for that calling is in the packing-house. Some men learn all they know from books; others from life; both kinds are narrow. The first are all theory; the second are all practice. It's the fellow who knows enough about practice to test his theories for blow-holes that gives the world a shove ahead, and finds a fair margin of profit in shoving it.

There's a chance for everything you have learned, from Latin to poetry, in the packing business, though we don't use much poetry here except in our street-car ads., and about the only time our products are given Latin names is when the State Board of Health condemns them. So I think

29

you'll find it safe to go short a little on the frills of education; if you want them bad enough you'll find a way to pick them up later, after business hours.

The main thing is to get a start along right lines, and that is what I sent you to college for. I didn't expect you to carry off all the education in sight—I knew you'd leave a little for the next fellow. But I wanted you to form good mental habits, just as I want you to have clean, straight physical ones. Because I was run through a threshing machine when I was a boy, and didn't begin to get the straw out of my hair till I was past thirty, I haven't any sympathy with a lot of these old fellows who go around bragging of their ignorance and saying that boys don't need to know anything except addition and the " best policy " brand of honesty.

We started in a mighty different world, and we were all ignorant together. The Lord let us in on the ground floor, gave us corner lots, and then started in to improve the adjacent property. We didn't have to know fractions to figure out our profits. Now a merchant needs astronomy to see them, and when he locates them they are out somewhere near the fifth decimal place. There are sixteen ounces to the pound still, but two of them are wrapping paper in a good many stores. And there're just as many chances for a fellow as ever, but they're a little gun shy, and you can't catch them by any such coarse method as putting salt on their tails.

Thirty years ago, you could take an old muzzle-loader and knock over plenty of ducks in the city limits, and Chicago wasn't Cook County then, either. You can get them still, but you've got to go to Kanka-kee and take a hammerless along. And when I started in the packing business it was all straight sailing—no frills—just turning hogs into hog meat—dry salt for the niggers down South and sugar-cured for the white folks up North. Everything else was sausage, or thrown away. But when we get through with a hog nowadays, he's scattered through a hundred different cans and packages, and he's all accounted for. What we used to throw away is our profit. It takes doctors, lawyers, engineers, poets, and I don't know what, to run the business, and I reckon that improvements which call for parsons will be creeping in next. Naturally, a young man who expects to hold his own when he is thrown in with a lot of men like these must be as clean and sharp as a hound's tooth, or some other fellow's simply going to eat him up.

The first college man I ever hired was old John Durham's son, Jim. That was a good many years ago when the house was a much smaller affair. Jim's father had a lot of money till he started out to buck the universe and corner wheat. And the boy took all the fancy courses and trimmings at college. The old man was mighty proud of

Jim. Wanted him to be a literary fellow. But old Durham found out what every one learns who gets his ambitions mixed up with number two red—that there's a heap of it lying around loose in the country. The bears did quick work and kept the cash wheat coming in so lively that one settling day half a dozen of us had to get under the market to keep it from going to everlasting smash.

That day made young Jim a candidate for a job. It didn't take him long to decide that the Lord would attend to keeping up the visible supply of poetry, and that he had better turn his attention to the stocks of mess pork. Next morning he was laying for me with a letter of introduction when I got to the office, and when he found that I wouldn't have a private secretary at any price, he applied for every other position on the premises right down to office boy. I told him I was sorry, but I couldn't do anything for him then; that we were

letting men go, but I'd keep him in mind,
and so on. The fact was that I didn't think
a fellow with Jim's training would be much
good, anyhow. But Jim hung on—said he'd
taken a fancy to the house, and wanted to
work for it. Used to call by about twice
a week to find out if anything had turned
up.

Finally, after about a month of this, he
wore me down so that I stopped him one
day as he was passing me on the street. I
thought I'd find out if he really was so
red-hot to work as he pretended to be; besides, I felt that perhaps I hadn't treated
the boy just right, as I had delivered quite
a jag of that wheat to his father myself.

" Hello, Jim," I called; " do you still
want that job? "

" Yes, sir," he answered, quick as lightning.

" Well, I tell you how it is, Jim," I said,
looking up at him—he was one of those
husky, lazy-moving six-footers—" I don't

see any chance in the office, but I understand they can use another good, strong
man in one of the loading gangs."

I thought that would settle Jim and let
me out, for it's no joke lugging beef, or
rolling barrels and tierces a hundred yards
or so to the cars. But Jim came right back
at me with, " Done. Who'll I report to? "

That sporty way of answering, as if he
was closing a bet, made me surer than ever
that he was not cut out for a butcher. But
I told him, and off he started hot-foot to
find the foreman. I sent word by another
route to see that he got plenty to do.

I forgot all about Jim until about three
months later, when his name was handed
up to me for a new place and a raise in
pay. It seemed that he had sort of abolished
his job. After he had been rolling barrels
a while, and the sport had ground down one
of his shoulders a couple of inches lower
than the other, he got to scheming around
for a way to make the work easier, and he

hit on an idea for a sort of overhead rail-road system, by which the barrels could be swung out of the storerooms and run right along into the cars, and two or three men do the work of a gang. It was just as I thought. Jim was lazy, but he had put the house in the way of saving so much money that I couldn't fire him. So I raised his salary, and made him an assistant time-keeper and checker. Jim kept at this for three or four months, until his feet began to hurt him, I guess, and then he was out of a job again. It seems he had heard something of a new machine for registering the men, that did away with most of the timekeepers except the fellows who watched the machines, and he kept after the Superin-tendent until he got him to put them in. Of course he claimed a raise again for ef-fecting such a saving, and we just had to allow it.

I was beginning to take an interest in Jim, so I brought him up into the office and set him to copying circular letters. We used to send out a raft of them to the trade. That was just before the general adoption of typewriters, when they were still in the experimental stage. But Jim hadn't been in the office plugging away at the letters for a month before he had the writer's cramp, and began nosing around again. The first thing I knew he was sicking the agents for the new typewriting machine on to me, and he kept them pounding away until they had made me give them a trial. Then it was all up with Mister Jim's job again. I raised his salary without his asking for it this time, and put him out on the road to introduce a new product that we were making—beef extract.

Jim made two trips without selling enough to keep them working overtime at the factory, and then he came into my office with a long story about how we were doing it all wrong. Said we ought to go for the consumer by advertising, and make the trade come to us, instead of chasing it up.

That was so like Jim that I just laughed at first; besides, that sort of advertising was a pretty new thing then, and I was one of the old-timers who didn't take any stock in it. But Jim just kept plugging away at me between trips, until finally I took him off the road and told him to go ahead and try it in a small way.

Jim pretty nearly scared me to death that first year. At last he had got into something that he took an interest in—spending money—and he just fairly wallowed in it. Used to lay awake nights, thinking up new ways of getting rid of the old man's profits. And he found them. Seemed as if I couldn't get away from Graham's Extract, and whenever I saw it I gagged, for I knew it was costing me money that wasn't coming back; but every time I started to draw in my horns Jim talked to me, and showed me

38

"*I put Jim Durham out on the road to introduce a new product.*"

where there was a fortune waiting for me just around the corner.

Graham's Extract started out by being something that you could make beef-tea out of—that was all. But before Jim had been fooling with it a month he had got his girl to think up a hundred different ways in which it could be used, and had advertised them all. It seemed there was nothing you could cook that didn't need a dash of it. He kept me between a chill and a sweat all the time. Sometimes, but not often, I just *had* to grin at his foolishness. I remember one picture he got out showing sixteen cows standing between something that looked like a letter-press, and telling how every pound or so of Graham's Extract contained the juice squeezed from a herd of steers. If an explorer started for the North Pole, Jim would send him a case of Extract, and then advertise that it was the great heat-maker for cold climates; and if some other

39

fellow started across Africa he sent *him* a case, too, and advertised what a bully drink it was served up with a little ice.

He broke out in a new place every day, and every time he broke out it cost the house money. Finally, I made up my mind to swallow the loss, and Mister Jim was just about to lose his job sure enough, when the orders for Extract began to look up, and he got a reprieve; then he began to make expenses, and he got a pardon; and finally a rush came that left him high and dry in a permanent place. Jim was all right in his way, but it was a new way, and I hadn't been broad-gauged enough to see that it was a better way.

That was where I caught the connection between a college education and business. I've always made it a rule to buy brains, and I've learned now that the better trained they are the faster they find reasons for getting their salaries raised. The fellow who hasn't had the training may be just as smart, but he's apt to paw the air when he's reaching for ideas.

I suppose you're asking why, if I'm so hot for education, I'm against this post-graduate course. But habits of thought ain't the only thing a fellow picks up at college.

I see you've been elected President of your class. I'm glad the boys aren't down on you, but while the most popular man in his class isn't always a failure in business, being as popular as that takes up a heap of time. I noticed, too, when you were home Easter, that you were running to sporty clothes and cigarettes. There's nothing criminal about either, but I don't hire sporty clerks at all, and the only part of the premises on which cigarette smoking is allowed is the fertilizer factory.

I simply mention this in passing. I have every confidence in your ultimate good sense, and I guess you'll see the point without my elaborating with a meat ax my reasons for thinking that you've had enough college for the present.

> Your affectionate father,
> JOHN GRAHAM.

No. 4

FROM John Graham, head of the house of Graham & Co., at the Union Stock Yards in Chicago, to his son, Pierrepont Graham, at the Waldorf-Astoria, in New York. Mr. Pierrepont has suggested the grand tour as a proper finish to his education.

IV

Dear Pierrepont: Your letter of the seventh twists around the point a good deal like a setter pup chasing his tail. But I gather from it that you want to spend a couple of months in Europe before coming on here and getting your nose in the bullring. Of course, you are your own boss now and you ought to be able to judge better than any one else how much time you have to waste, but it seems to me, on general principles, that a young man of twenty-two, who is physically and mentally sound, and who hasn't got a dollar and has never earned one, can't be getting on somebody's pay-roll too quick. And in this connection it is only fair to tell you that I have instructed the cashier to discontinue your allowance after July 15. That gives you two weeks for a vacation—enough to make a sick boy well, or a lazy one lazier.

45

I hear a good deal about men who won't take vacations, and who kill themselves by overwork, but it's usually worry or whiskey. It's not what a man does during working-hours, but after them, that breaks down his health. A fellow and his business should be bosom friends in the office and sworn enemies out of it. A clear mind is one that is swept clean of business at six o'clock every night and isn't opened up for it again until after the shutters are taken down next morning.

Some fellows leave the office at night and start out to whoop it up with the boys, and some go home to sit up with their troubles —they're both in bad company. They're the men who are always needing vacations, and never getting any good out of them. What every man does need once a year is a change of work—that is, if he has been curved up over a desk for fifty weeks and subsisting on birds and burgundy, he ought to take to fishing for a living and try bacon and eggs, with a little spring water, for dinner. But coming from Harvard to the packing-house will give you change enough this year to keep you in good trim, even if you didn't have a fortnight's leeway to run loose.

You will always find it a safe rule to take a thing just as quick as it is offered—especially a job. It is never easy to get one except when you don't want it; but when you have to get work, and go after it with a gun, you'll find it as shy as an old crow that every farmer in the county has had a shot at.

When I was a young fellow and out of a place, I always made it a rule to take the first job that offered, and to use it for bait. You can catch a minnow with a worm, and a bass will take your minnow. A good fat bass will tempt an otter, and then you've got something worth skinning. Of course, there's no danger of your not being able to get a job with the house—in fact, there is no real way in which you can escape getting

47

one; but I don't like to see you shy off every time the old man gets close to you with the halter.

I want you to learn right at the outset not to play with the spoon before you take the medicine. Putting off an easy thing makes it hard, and putting off a hard one makes it impossible. Procrastination is the longest word in the language, but there's only one letter between its ends when they occupy their proper places in the alphabet.

Old Dick Stover, for whom I once clerked in Indiana, was the worst hand at procrastinating that I ever saw. Dick was a powerful hearty eater, and no one ever loved meal-time better, but he used to keep turning over in bed mornings for just another wink and staving off getting up, until finally his wife combined breakfast and dinner on him, and he only got two meals a day. He was a mighty religious man, too, but he got to putting off saying his prayers until after he was in bed, and then he would keep passing them along until his mind was clear of worldly things, and in the end he would drop off to sleep without saying them at all. What between missing the Sunday morning service and never being seen on his knees, the first thing Dick knew he was turned out of the church. He had a pretty good business when I first went with him, but he would keep putting off firing his bad clerks until they had lit out with the petty cash; and he would keep putting off raising the salaries of his good ones until his competitor had hired them away. Finally, he got so that he wouldn't discount his bills, even when he had the money; and when they came due he would give notes so as to keep from paying out his cash a little longer. Running a business on those lines is, of course, equivalent to making a will in favor of the sheriff and committing suicide so that he can inherit. The last I heard of Dick he was ninety-three years old and just about to die. That was ten years ago, and I'll bet he's living yet. I simply mention Dick in passing as an instance of how habits rule a man's life.

There is one excuse for every mistake a man can make, but only one. When a fellow makes the same mistake twice he's got to throw up both hands and own up to carelessness or cussedness. Of course, I knew that you would make a fool of yourself pretty often when I sent you to college, and I haven't been disappointed. But I expected you to narrow down the number of combinations possible by making a different sort of a fool of yourself every time. That is the important thing, unless a fellow has too lively an imagination, or has none at all. You are bound to try this European foolishness sooner or later, but if you will wait a few years, you will approach it in an entirely different spirit—and you will come back with a good deal of respect for the people who have sense enough to stay at home.

50

*"Old Dick Stover was the worst hand
at procrastinating that I ever saw."*

I piece out from your letter that you expect a few months on the other side will sort of put a polish on you. I don't want to seem pessimistic, but I have seen hundreds of boys graduate from college and go over with the same idea, and they didn't bring back a great deal except a few trunks of badly fitting clothes. Seeing the world is like charity—it covers a multitude of sins, and, like charity, it ought to begin at home.

Culture is not a matter of a change of climate. You'll hear more about Browning to the square foot in the Mississippi Valley than you will in England. And there's as much Art talk on the Lake front as in the Latin Quarter. It may be a little different, but it's there.

I went to Europe once myself. I was pretty raw when I left Chicago, and I was pretty sore when I got back. Coming and going I was simply sick. In London, for the first time in my life, I was taken for an

51

easy thing. Every time I went into a store there was a bull movement. The clerks all knocked off their regular work and started in to mark up prices.

They used to tell me that they didn't have any gold-brick men over there. So they don't. They deal in pictures—old masters, they call them. I bought two—you know the ones—those hanging in the waiting-room at the stock yards; and when I got back I found out that they had been painted by a measly little fellow who went to Paris to study art, after Bill Harris had found out that he was no good as a settling clerk. I keep 'em to remind myself that there's no fool like an old American fool when he gets this picture paresis.

The fellow who tried to fit me out with a coat-of-arms didn't find me so easy. I picked mine when I first went into business for myself—a charging steer—and it's registered at Washington. It's my trade-mark, of course, and that's the only coat-of-arms an American merchant has any business with. It's penetrated to every quarter of the globe in the last twenty years, and every soldier in the world has carried it—in his knapsack.

I take just as much pride in it as the fellow who inherits his and can't find any place to put it, except on his carriage door and his letter-head—and it's a heap more profitable. It's got so now that every jobber in the trade knows that it stands for good quality, and that's all any Englishman's coat-of-arms can stand for. Of course, an American's can't stand for anything much—generally it's the burned-in-the-skin brand of a snob.

After the way some of the descendants of the old New York Dutchmen with the hoe and the English general storekeepers have turned out, I sometimes feel a little uneasy about what my great-grandchildren may

53

do, but we'll just stick to the trade-mark and try to live up to it while the old man's in the saddle.

I simply mention these things in a general way. I have no fears for you after you've been at work for a few years, and have struck an average between the packing-house and Harvard; then if you want to graze over a wider range it can't hurt you. But for the present you will find yourself pretty busy trying to get into the winning class.

Your affectionate father,
JOHN GRAHAM.

FROM John Graham, head of the house of Graham & Co., at the Union Stock Yards in Chicago, to his son, Pierrepont Graham, at Lake Moosgatchemawamuc, in the Maine woods. Mr. Pierrepont has written to his father withdrawing his suggestion.

V

Dear Pierrepont: Yours of the fourth has the right ring, and it says more to the number of words used than any letter that I have ever received from you. I remember reading once that some fellows use language to conceal thought; but it's been my experience that a good many more use it *instead* of thought.

A business man's conversation should be regulated by fewer and simpler rules than any other function of the human animal. They are:

Have something to say.

Say it.

Stop talking.

Beginning before you know what you want to say and keeping on after you have said it lands a merchant in a lawsuit or the poorhouse, and the first is a short cut to the second. I maintain a legal department here, and it costs a lot of money, but it's to keep me from going to law.

It's all right when you are calling on a girl or talking with friends after dinner to run a conversation like a Sunday-school excursion, with stops to pick flowers; but in the office your sentences should be the shortest distance possible between periods. Cut out the introduction and the peroration, and stop before you get to secondly. You've got to preach short sermons to catch sinners; and deacons won't believe they need long ones themselves. Give fools the first and women the last word. The meat's always in the middle of the sandwich. Of course, a little butter on either side of it doesn't do any harm if it's intended for a man who likes butter.

Remember, too, that it's easier to look wise than to talk wisdom. Say less than the other fellow and listen more than you talk; for when a man's listening he isn't telling on himself and he's flattering the fel-

low who is. Give most men a good listener
and most women enough note-paper and
they'll tell all they know. Money talks—but
not unless its owner has a loose tongue, and
then its remarks are always offensive. Poverty talks, too, but nobody wants to hear
what it has to say.

I simply mention these things in passing
because I'm afraid you're apt to be the
fellow who's doing the talking; just as I'm
a little afraid that you're sometimes like
the hungry drummer at the dollar-a-day
house—inclined to kill your appetite by eating the cake in the centre of the table before the soup comes on.

Of course, I'm glad to see you swing into
line and show the proper spirit about coming on here and going to work; but you
mustn't get yourself all "het up" before
you take the plunge, because you're bound
to find the water pretty cold at first. I've
seen a good many young fellows pass
through and out of this office. The first

week a lot of them go to work they're in a
sweat for fear they'll be fired; and the second week for fear they won't be. By the
third, a boy that's no good has learned just
how little work he can do and keep his job;
while the fellow who's got the right stuff
in him is holding down his own place with
one hand and beginning to reach for the
job just ahead of him with the other. I
don't mean that he's neglecting his work;
but he's beginning to take notice, and that's
a mighty hopeful sign in either a young
clerk or a young widow.

You've got to handle the first year of
your business life about the way you would
a trotting horse. Warm up a little before
going to the post—not enough to be in a
sweat, but just enough to be limber and
eager. Never start off at a gait that you
can't improve on, but move along strong
and well in hand to the quarter. Let out a
notch there, but take it calm enough up to
the half not to break, and hard enough not

to fall back into the ruck. At the three-quarters you ought to be going fast enough to poke your nose out of the other fellow's dust, and running like the Limited in the stretch. Keep your eyes to the front all the time, and you won't be so apt to shy at the little things by the side of the track. Head up, tail over the dashboard—that's the way the winners look in the old pictures of Maud S. and Dexter and Jay-Eye-See. And that's the way I want to see you swing by the old man at the end of the year, when we hoist the numbers of the fellows who are good enough to promote and pick out the salaries which need a little sweetening.

I've always taken a good deal of stock in what you call " Blood-will-tell " if you're a Methodist, or " Heredity " if you're a Unitarian; and I don't want you to come along at this late day and disturb my religious beliefs. A man's love for his children and his pride are pretty badly snarled up in this world, and he can't always pick them apart. I think a heap of you and a heap of the house, and I want to see you get along well together. To do that you must start right. It's just as necessary to make a good first impression in business as in courting. You'll read a good deal about "love at first sight" in novels, and there may be something in it for all I know; but I'm dead certain there's no such thing as love at first sight in business. A man's got to keep company a long time, and come early and stay late and sit close, before he can get a girl or a job worth having. There's nothing comes without calling in this world, and after you've called you've generally got to go and fetch it yourself.

Our bright young men have discovered how to make a pretty good article of potted chicken, and they don't need any help from hens, either; and you can smell the clover in our butterine if you've developed the poetic side of your nose; but none of the boys have been able to discover anything

"*Charlie Chase told me he was President of the Klondike Exploring, Gold Prospecting and Immigration Company.*"

that will pass as a substitute for work, even in a boarding-house, though I'll give some of them credit for having tried pretty hard.

I remember when I was selling goods for old Josh Jennings, back in the sixties, and had rounded up about a thousand in a savings-bank—a mighty hard thousand, that came a dollar or so at a time, and every dollar with a little bright mark where I had bit it—I roomed with a dry-goods clerk named Charlie Chase. Charlie had a hankering to be a rich man; but somehow he could never see any connection between that hankering and his counter, except that he'd hint to me sometimes about an heiress who used to squander her father's money shamefully for the sake of having Charlie wait on her. But when it came to getting rich outside the dry-goods business and getting rich in a hurry, Charlie was the man.

Along about Tuesday night—he was paid on Saturday—he'd stay at home and begin to scheme. He'd commence at eight o'clock and start a magazine, maybe, and before midnight he'd be turning away subscribers because his preses couldn't print a big enough edition. Or perhaps he wouldn't feel literary that night, and so he'd invent a system for speculating in wheat and go on pyramiding his purchases till he'd made the best that Cheops did look like a five-cent plate of ice cream. All he ever needed was a few hundred for a starter, and to get that he'd decide to let me in on the ground floor. I want to say right here that whenever any one offers to let you in on the ground floor it's a pretty safe rule to take the elevator to the roof garden. I never exactly refused to lend Charlie the capital he needed, but we generally compromised on half a dollar next morning, when he was in a hurry to make the store to keep from getting docked.

He dropped by the office last week, a little bent and seedy, but all in a glow and trembling with excitement in the old way. Told me he was President of the Klondike

64

Exploring, Gold Prospecting and Immigration Company, with a capital of ten millions. I guessed that he was the board of directors and the capital stock and the exploring and the prospecting and the immigrating, too— everything, in fact, except the business card he'd sent in; for Charlie always had a gift for nosing out printers who'd trust him. Said that for the sake of old times he'd let me have a few thousand shares at fifty cents, though they would go to par in a year. In the end we compromised on a loan of ten dollars, and Charlie went away happy.

The swamps are full of razor-backs like Charlie, fellows who'd rather make a million a night in their heads than five dollars a day in cash. I have always found it cheaper to lend a man of that build a little money than to hire him. As a matter of fact, I have never known a fellow who was smart enough to think for the house days and for himself nights. A man who tries that is usually a pretty poor thinker, and he isn't much good to either; but if there's any choice the house gets the worst of it.

I simply mention these little things in a general way. If you can take my word for some of them you are going to save yourself a whole lot of trouble. There are others which I don't speak of because life is too short and because it seems to afford a fellow a heap of satisfaction to pull the trigger for himself to see if it is loaded; and a lesson learned at the muzzle has the virtue of never being forgotten.

You report to Milligan at the yards at eight sharp on the fifteenth. You'd better figure on being here on the fourteenth, because Milligan's a pretty touchy Irishman, and I may be able to give you a point or two that will help you to keep on his mellow side. He's apt to feel a little sore at taking on in his department a man whom he hasn't passed on.

Your affectionate father,
JOHN GRAHAM.

No. 6

FROM John Graham, en route to Texas, to Pierrepont Graham, care of Graham & Co., Union Stock Yards, Chicago. Mr. Pierrepont has, entirely without intention, caused a little confusion in the mails, and it has come to his father's notice in the course of business.

VI

Dear Pierrepont: Perhaps it's just as well that I had to hurry last night to make my train, and so had no time to tell you some things that are laying mighty heavy on my mind this morning.

Jim Donnelly, of the Donnelly Provision Company, came into the office in the afternoon, with a fool grin on his fat face, to tell me that while he appreciated a note which he had just received in one of the firm's envelopes, beginning " Dearest," and containing an invitation to the theatre to-morrow night, it didn't seem to have any real bearing on his claim for shortage on the last carload of sweet pickled hams he had bought from us.

Of course, I sent for Milligan and went for him pretty rough for having a mailing clerk so no-account as to be writing personal letters in office hours, and such a blunderer as to mix them up with the firm's correspondence. Milligan just stood there like a dumb Irishman and let me get through and go back and cuss him out all over again, with some trimmings that I had forgotten the first time, before he told me that you were the fellow who had made the bull. Naturally, I felt pretty foolish, and, while I tried to pass it off with something about your still being green and raw, the ice was mighty thin, and you had the old man running tiddledies.

It didn't make me feel any sweeter about the matter to hear that when Milligan went for you, and asked what you supposed Donnelly would think of that sort of business, you told him to " consider the feelings of the girl who got our brutal refusal to allow a claim for a few hundredweight of hams."

I haven't any special objection to your writing to girls and telling them that they are the real sugar-cured article, for, after

70

all, if you overdo it, it's your breach-of-promise suit, but you must write before eight or after six. I have bought the stretch between those hours. Your time is money—my money—and when you take half an hour of it for your own purposes, that is just a petty form of petty larceny.

Milligan tells me that you are quick to learn, and that you can do a powerful lot of work when you've a mind to; but he adds that it's mighty seldom your mind takes that particular turn. Your attention may be on the letters you are addressing, or you may be in a comatose condition mentally; he never quite knows until the returns come from the dead-letter office.

A man can't have his head pumped out like a vacuum pan, or stuffed full of odds and ends like a bologna sausage, and do his work right. It doesn't make any difference how mean and trifling the thing he's doing may seem, that's the big thing and the only thing for him just then. Business is like oil—it won't mix with anything but business.

You can resolve everything in the world, even a great fortune, into atoms. And the fundamental principles which govern the handling of postage stamps and of millions are exactly the same. They are the common law of business, and the whole practice of commerce is founded on them. They are so simple that a fool can't learn them; so hard that a lazy man won't.

Boys are constantly writing me for advice about how to succeed, and when I send them my receipt they say that I am dealing out commonplace generalities. Of course I am, but that's what the receipt calls for, and if a boy will take these commonplace generalities and knead them into his job, the mixture'll be cake.

Once a fellow's got the primary business virtues cemented into his character, he's safe to build on. But when a clerk crawls

"Jim Donnelly of the Donnelly Provision Company came into my office with
a fool grin on his fat face."

into the office in the morning like a sick setter pup, and leaps from his stool at night
with the spring of a tiger, I'm a little afraid
that if I sent him off to take charge of a
branch house he wouldn't always be around
when customers were. He's the sort of a
chap who would hold back the sun an hour
every morning and have it gain two every
afternoon if the Lord would give him the
same discretionary powers that He gave
Joshua. And I have noticed that he's the
fellow who invariably takes a timekeeper
as an insult. He's pretty numerous in business offices; in fact, if the glance of the
human eye could affect a clockface in the
same way that a man's country cousins affect their city welcome, I should have to buy
a new timepiece for the office every morning.

I remember when I was a boy, we used to
have a pretty lively camp-meeting every
summer, and Elder Hoover, who was accounted a powerful exhorter in our parts,
would wrastle with the sinners and the

backsliders. There was one old chap in the
town—Bill Budlong—who took a heap of
pride in being the simon pure cuss. Bill
was always the last man to come up to the
mourners' bench at the camp-meeting and
the first one to backslide when it was over.
Used to brag around about what a hold
Satan had on him and how his sin was the
original brand, direct from Adam, put up
in cans to keep, and the can-opener lost.
Doc Hoover would get the whole town safe
in the fold and then have to hold extra meetings for a couple of days to snake in that
miserable Bill; but, in the end, he always
got religion and got it hard. For a month or
two afterward, he'd make the chills run
down the backs of us children in prayer-
meeting, telling how he had probably been
the triflingest and orneriest man alive before
he was converted. Then, along toward hog-
killing time, he'd backslide, and go around
bragging that he was standing so close to

the mouth of the pit that his whiskers smelt of brimstone.

He kept this up for about ten years, getting vainer and vainer of his staying qualities, until one summer, when the Elder had rounded up all the likeliest sinners in the bunch, he announced that the meetings were over for that year.

You never saw a sicker-looking man than Bill when he heard that there wasn't going to be any extra session for him. He got up and said he reckoned another meeting would fetch him; that he sort of felt the clutch of old Satan loosening; but Doc Hoover was firm. Then Bill begged to have a special deacon told off to wrastle with him, but Doc wouldn't listen to that. Said he'd been wasting time enough on him for ten years to save a county, and he had just about made up his mind to let him try his luck by himself; that what he really needed more than religion was common-sense and a con-

75

viction that time in this world was too valuable to be frittered away. If he'd get that
in his head he didn't think he'd be so apt to
trifle with eternity; and if he didn't get it,
religion wouldn't be of any special use to
him.

A big merchant finds himself in Doc
Hoover's fix pretty often. There are too
many likely young sinners in his office to
make it worth while to bother long with the
Bills. Very few men are worth wasting
time on beyond a certain point, and that
point is soon reached with a fellow who
doesn't show any signs of wanting to help.
Naturally, a green man always comes to a
house in a pretty subordinate position, and
it isn't possible to make so much noise with
a firecracker as with a cannon. But you
can tell a good deal by what there is left of
the boy, when you come to inventory him on
the fifth of July, whether he'll be safe to
trust with a cannon next year.

It isn't the little extra money that you may make for the house by learning the fundamental business virtues which counts so much as it is the effect that it has on your character and that of those about you, and especially on the judgment of the old man when he's casting around for the fellow to fill the vacancy just ahead of you. He's pretty apt to pick some one who keeps separate ledger accounts for work and for fun, who gives the house sixteen ounces to the pound, and, on general principles, to pass by the one who is late at the end where he ought to be early, and early at the end where he ought to be late.

I simply mention these things in passing, but, frankly, I am afraid that you have a streak of the Bill in you; and you can't be a good clerk, let alone a partner, until you get it out. I try not to be narrow when I'm weighing up a young fellow, and to allow for soakage and leakage, and then to throw

77

in a little for good feeling; but I don't trade with a man whom I find deliberately marking up the weights on me.

This is a fine country we're running through, but it's a pity that it doesn't raise more hogs. It seems to take a farmer a long time to learn that the best way to sell his corn is on the hoof.

Your affectionate father,

JOHN GRAHAM.

P. S. I just had to allow Donnelly his claim on those hams, though I was dead sure our weights were right, and it cost the house sixty dollars. But your fool letter took all the snap out of our argument. I get hot every time I think of it.

No. 7

FROM John Graham, at the Omaha Branch of Graham & Co., to Pierrepont Graham, at the Union Stock Yards, Chicago. Mr. Pierrepont hasn't found the methods of the worthy Milligan altogether to his liking, and he has commented rather freely on them.

VII

Dear Pierrepont: Yours of the 30th ultimo strikes me all wrong. I don't like to hear you say that you can't work under Milligan or any other man, for it shows a fundamental weakness. And then, too, the house isn't interested in knowing how you like your boss, but in how he likes you.

I understand all about Milligan. He's a cross, cranky old Irishman with a temper tied up in bow-knots, who prods his men with the bull-stick six days a week and schemes to get them salary raises on the seventh, when he ought to be listening to the sermon; who puts the black-snake on a clerk's hide when he sends a letter to Oshkosh that ought to go to Kalamazoo, and begs him off when the old man wants to have him fired for it. Altogether he's a hard, crabbed, generous, soft-hearted, loyal, bully old boy, who's been with the house since we took down the shutters for the first time, and who's going to stay with it till we put them up for the last time.

But all that apart, you want to get it firmly fixed in your mind that you're going to have a Milligan over you all your life, and if it isn't a Milligan it will be a Jones or a Smith, and the chances are that you'll find them both harder to get along with than this old fellow. And if it isn't Milligan or Jones or Smith, and you ain't a butcher, but a parson or a doctor, or even the President of the United States, it'll be a way-back deacon, or the undertaker, or the machine. There isn't any such thing as being your own boss in this world unless you're a tramp, and then there's the constable.

Like the old man if you can, but give him no cause to dislike you. Keep your self-respect at any cost, and your upper lip stiff at the same figure. Criticism can properly come only from above, and whenever you discover that your boss is no good you may rest easy that the man who pays his salary shares your secret. Learn to give back a bit from the base-burner, to let the village fathers get their feet on the fender and the sawdust box in range, and you'll find them making a little room for you in turn. Old men have tender feet, and apologies are poor salve for aching corns. Remember that when you're in the right you can afford to keep your temper, and that when you're in the wrong you can't afford to lose it.

When you've got an uncertain cow it's all O. K. to tie a figure eight in her tail, if you ain't thirsty, and it's excitement you're after; but if you want peace and her nine quarts, you will naturally approach her from the side, and say, So-boss, in about the same tone that you would use if you were asking your best girl to let you hold her hand.

Of course, you want to be sure of your natural history facts and learn to distin-

guish between a cow that's a kicker, but
whose intentions are good if she's approached with proper respect, and a hooker,
who is vicious on general principles, and
any way you come at her. There's never
any use fooling with an animal of that sort,
brute or human. The only safe place is the
other side of the fence or the top of the
nearest tree.

When I was clerking in Missouri, a fellow
named Jeff Hankins moved down from Wisconsin and bought a little clearing just outside the town. Jeff was a good talker, but a
bad listener, and so we learned a heap about
how things were done in Wisconsin, but he
didn't pick up much information about the
habits of our Missouri fauna. When it came
to cows, he had had a liberal education and
he made out all right, but by and by it got
on to ploughing time and Jeff naturally
bought a mule—a little moth-eaten cuss,
with sad, dreamy eyes and droopy, wiggly-
woggly ears that swung in a circle as easy

*" Bill Budlong was always the last
man to come up to the mourners' bench."*

as if they ran on ball-bearings. Her owner didn't give her a very good character, but Jeff was too busy telling how much he knew about horses to pay much attention to what anybody was saying about mules. So finally the seller turned her loose in Jeff's lot, told him he wouldn't have any trouble catching her if he approached her right, and hurried off out of range.

Next morning at sunup Jeff picked out a bridle and started off whistling Buffalo Gals—he was a powerful pretty whistler and could do the Mocking Bird with variations—to catch the mule and begin his plowing. The animal was feeding as peaceful as a water-color picture, and she didn't budge; but when Jeff began to get nearer, her ears dropped back along her neck as if they had lead in them. He knew that symptom and so he closed up kind of cautious, aiming for her at right angles and gurgling, "Muley, muley, here muley; that's a good muley," sort of soothing and caressing-like.

Still she didn't stir and Jeff got right up to her and put one arm over her back and began to reach forward with the bridle, when something happened. He never could explain just what it was, but we judged from the marks on his person that the mule had reached forward and kicked the seat of his trousers with one of her prehensile hind feet; and had reached back and caught him on the last button of his waistcoat with one of her limber fore feet; and had twisted around her elastic neck and bit off a mouthful of his hair. When Jeff regained consciousness, he reckoned that the only really safe way to approach a mule was to drop on it from a balloon.

I simply mention this little incident as an example of the fact that there are certain animals with which the Lord didn't intend white men to fool. And you will find that, as a rule, the human varieties of them are not the fellows who go for you rough-shod, like Milligan, when you're wrong. It's when you come across one of those gentlemen who have more oil in their composition than any two-legged animal has a right to have, that you should be on the lookout for concealed deadly weapons.

I don't mean that you should distrust a man who is affable and approachable, but you want to learn to distinguish between him and one who is too affable and too approachable. The adverb makes the difference between a good and a bad fellow. The bunco men aren't all at the county fair, and they don't all operate with the little shells and the elusive pea. When a packer has learned all that there is to learn about quadrupeds, he knows only one-eighth of his business; the other seven-eighths, and the important seven-eighths, has to do with the study of bipeds.

I dwell on this because I am a little disappointed that you should have made such a mistake in sizing up Milligan. He isn't the brightest man in the office, but he is loyal to me and to the house, and when you have been in business as long as I have you will be inclined to put a pretty high value on loyalty. It is the one commodity that hasn't any market value, and it's the one that you can't pay too much for. You can trust any number of men with your money, but mighty few with your reputation. Half the men who are with the house on pay day are against it the other six.

A good many young fellows come to me looking for jobs, and start in by telling me what a mean house they have been working for; what a cuss to get along with the senior partner was; and how little show a bright, progressive clerk had with him. I never get very far with a critter of that class, because I know that he wouldn't like me or the house if he came to work for us.

I don't know anything that a young business man ought to keep more entirely to himself than his dislikes, unless it is his likes. It's generally expensive to have either, but it's bankruptcy to tell about them. It's all right to say nothing about the dead but good, but it's better to apply the rule to the living, and especially to the house which is paying your salary.

Just one word before I close, as old Doc Hoover used to say, when he was coming into the stretch, but still a good ways off from the benediction. I have noticed that you are inclined to be a little chesty and starchy around the office. Of course, it's good business, when a fellow hasn't much behind his forehead, to throw out his chest and attract attention to his shirt-front. But as you begin to meet the men who have done something that makes them worth meeting you will find that there are no " keep off the grass " or " beware of the dog " signs around their premises, and that they don't motion to the orchestra to play slow music while they talk.

Superiority makes every man feel its equal. It is courtesy without condescension; affability without familiarity; self-sufficiency without selfishness; simplicity without snide. It weighs sixteen ounces to the pound without the package, and it doesn't need a four-colored label to make it go.

We are coming home from here. I am a little disappointed in the showing that this house has been making. Pound for pound it is not getting nearly so much out of its hogs as we are in Chicago. I don't know just where the leak is, but if they don't do better next month I am coming back here with a shotgun, and there's going to be a pretty heavy mortality among our head men.

Your affectionate father,

JOHN GRAHAM.

No. 8

FROM John Graham, at Hot Springs, Arkansas, to his son, Pierrepont, at the Union Stock Yards in Chicago. Mr. Pierrepont has just been promoted from the mailing to the billing desk and, in consequence, his father is feeling rather "mellow" toward him.

VIII

Dear Pierrepont: They've run me through the scalding vats here till they've pretty nearly taken all the hair off my hide, but that or something else has loosened up my joints so that they don't squeak any more when I walk. The doctor says he'll have my rheumatism cured in thirty days, so I guess you can expect me home in about a fortnight. For he's the breed of doctor that is always two weeks ahead of his patients' condition when they're poor, and two weeks behind it when they're rich. He calls himself a specialist, which means that it costs me ten dollars every time he has a look in at my tongue, against two that I would pay the family doctor for gratifying his curiosity. But I guess this specialist business is about the only outlet for marketing the surplus of young doctors.

Reminds me of the time when we were

piling up canned corned beef in stock faster than people would eat it, and a big drought happened along in Texas and began driving the canners in to the packing-house quicker than we could tuck them away in tin. Jim Durham tried to "stimulate the consumption," as he put it, by getting out a nice little booklet called, "A Hundred Dainty Dishes from a Can," and telling how to work off corned beef on the family in various disguises; but, after he had schemed out ten different combinations, the other ninety turned out to be corned-beef hash. So that was no use.

But one day we got together and had a nice, fancy, appetizing label printed, and we didn't economize on the gilt—a picture of a steer so fat that he looked as if he'd break his legs if they weren't shored up pretty quick with props, and with blue ribbons tied to his horns. We labeled it "Blue Ribbon Beef—For Fancy Family Trade," and charged an extra ten cents a dozen for the cans on which that special label was pasted. Of course, people just naturally wanted it.

There's nothing helps convince some men that a thing has merit like a little gold on the label. And it's pretty safe to bet that if a fellow needs a six or seven-syllabled word to describe his profession, he's a corn doctor when you come to look him up in the dictionary. And then you'll generally find him in the back part of the book where they tuck away the doubtful words.

But that isn't what I started out to say. I want to tell you that I was very, very glad to learn from your letter that you had been promoted to the billing desk. I have felt all along that when you got a little of the nonsense tried out of you there would be a residue of common-sense, and I am glad to have your boss back up my judgment. There's two things you just naturally don't expect from human nature—that the widow's tombstone estimate of the departed, on which she is trying to convince the neighbors against their better judgment that he went to Heaven, and the father's estimate of the son, on which he is trying to pass him along into a good salary, will be conservative.

I had that driven into my mind and spiked down when I hired the widow's son a few years ago. His name was Clarence—Clarence St. Clair Hicks—and his father used to keep books for me when he wasn't picking the winners at Washington Park or figuring out the batting averages of the Chicagos. He was one of those quick men who always have their books posted up half an hour before closing time for three weeks of the month, and spend the evenings of the fourth hunting up the eight cents that they are out on the trial balance. When he died his wife found that his life insurance had lapsed the month before, and so she brought Clarence down to the office and asked me to give him a job.

Clarence wasn't exactly a pretty boy; in fact, he looked to me like another of his father's bad breaks; but his mother seemed to think a heap of him. I learned that he would have held the belt in his Sunday-school for long-distance verse-reciting if the mother of one of the other boys hadn't fixed the superintendent, and that it had taken a general conspiracy of the teachers in his day-school to keep him from walking off with the good-conduct medal.

I couldn't just reconcile those statements with Clarence's face, but I accepted him at par and had him passed along to the head errand boy. His mother cried a little when she saw him marched off, and asked me to see that he was treated kindly and wasn't bullied by the bigger boys, because he had been " raised a pet."

A number of unusual things happened in the offices that morning, and the head office boy thought Clarence might be able to explain some of them, but he had an alibi ready every time—even when a bookkeeper found the vault filled with cigarette smoke and Clarence in it hunting for something he couldn't describe. But as he was a new boy, no one was disposed to bear down on him very hard, so his cigarettes were taken away from him and he was sent back to his bench with a warning that he had used up all his explanations.

Along toward noon, a big Boston customer came in with his little boy—a nice, plump, stall-fed youngster, with black velvet pants and hair that was just a little longer than was safe in the stock-yards district. And while we were talking business, the kid wandered off to the coat-room, where the errand boys were eating lunch, which was a pretty desperate place for a boy with velvet pants on to go.

As far as we could learn from Willie when he came out of his convulsions, the boys had been very polite to him and had insisted on his joining in a new game which

" Clarence looked to me like another of his father's bad breaks."

Clarence had just invented, called playing pig-sticker. And, because he was company, Clarence told him that he could be the pig. Willie didn't know just what being the pig meant, but, as he told his father, it didn't sound very nice and he was afraid he wouldn't like it. So he tried to pass along the honor to some one else, but Clarence insisted that it was " hot stuff to be the pig," and before Willie could rightly judge what was happening to him, one end of a rope had been tied around his left ankle and the other end had been passed over a transom bar, and he was dangling headforemost in the air, while Clarence threatened his jugular with a lath sword. That was when he let out the yell which brought his father and me on the jump and scattered the boys all over the stock yards.

Willie's father canceled his bologna contract and marched off muttering something about " degrading surroundings brutalizing the young; " and Clarence's mother wrote me that I was a bad old man who had held her husband down all his life and now wouldn't give her son a show. For, naturally, after that little incident, I had told the boy who had been raised a pet that he had better go back to the menagerie.

I simply mention Clarence in passing as an instance of why I am a little slow to trust my judgment on my own. I have always found that, whenever I thought a heap of anything I owned, there was nothing like getting the other fellow's views expressed in figures; and the other fellow is usually a pessimist when he's buying. The lady on the dollar is the only woman who hasn't any sentiment in her make-up. And if you really want a look at the solid facts of a thing you must strain off the sentiment first.

I put you under Milligan to get a view of you through his eyes. If he says that you are good enough to be a billing clerk, and to draw twelve dollars a week, I guess there's no doubt about it. For he's one of those men that never show any real enthusiasm except when they're cussing.

Naturally, it's a great satisfaction to see a streak or two of business ability beginning to show under the knife, because when it comes closing time for me it will make it a heap easier to know that some one who bears the name will take down the shutters in the morning.

Boys are a good deal like the pups that fellows sell on street corners—they don't always turn out as represented. You buy a likely setter pup and raise a spotted coach dog from it, and the promising son of an honest butcher is just as like as not to turn out a poet or a professor. I want to say in passing that I have no real prejudice against poets, but I believe that, if you're going to be a Milton, there's nothing like being a mute, inglorious one, as some fellow who was a little sore on the poetry business once put it. Of course, a packer who understands something about the versatility of cottonseed oil need never turn down orders for lard because the run of hogs is light, and a father who understands human nature can turn out an imitation parson from a boy whom the Lord intended to go on the Board of Trade. But on general principles it's best to give your cottonseed oil a Latin name and to market it on its merits, and to let your boy follow his bent, even if it leads him into the wheat pit. If a fellow has got poetry in him it's bound to come out sooner or later in the papers or the street cars; and the longer you keep it bottled up the harder it comes, and the longer it takes the patient to recover. There's no easier way to cure foolishness than to give a man leave to be foolish. And the only way to show a fellow that he's chosen the wrong business is to let him try it. If it really is the wrong thing you won't have to argue with him to quit, and if it isn't you haven't any right to.

Speaking of bull-pups that turned out to be terriers naturally calls to mind the case of my old friend Jeremiah Simpkins' son. There isn't a solider man in the Boston leather trade than Jeremiah, nor a bigger scamp that the law can't touch than his son Ezra. There isn't an ounce of real meanness in Ezra's whole body, but he's just naturally and unintentionally a maverick. When he came out of college his father thought that a few years' experience in the hide department of Graham & Co. would be a good thing for him before he tackled the leather business. So I wrote to send him on and I would give him a job, supposing, of course, that I was getting a yearling of the steady, old, reliable Simpkins strain.

I was a little uneasy when Ezra reported, because he didn't just look as if he had had a call to leather. He was a tall, spare New Englander, with one of those knobby foreheads which has been pushed out by the overcrowding of the brain, or bulged by the thickening of the skull, according as you like or dislike the man. His manners were easy or familiar by the same standard. He told me right at the start that, while he didn't know just what he wanted to do, he was dead sure that it wasn't the leather business. It seemed that he had said the same thing to his father and that the old man had answered, " Tut, tut," and told him to forget it and to learn hides.

Simpkins learned all that he wanted to know about the packing industry in thirty days, and I learned all that I wanted to know about Ezra in the same time. Pork-packing seemed to be the only thing that he wasn't interested in. I got his resignation one day just five minutes before the one which I was having written out for him was ready; for I will do Simpkins the justice to say that there was nothing slow about him. He and his father split up, temporarily, over it, and, of course, it cost me the old man's trade and friendship. I want to say right here that the easiest way in the world to make enemies is to hire friends.

I lost sight of Simpkins for a while, and then he turned up at the office one morning as friendly and familiar as ever. Said he was a reporter and wanted to interview me on the December wheat deal. Of course, I wouldn't talk on that, but I gave him a little fatherly advice—told him he would sleep in a hall bedroom all his life if he didn't quit his foolishness and go back to his father, though I didn't really believe it. He thanked me and went off and wrote a column about what I might have said about December wheat, and somehow gave the impression that I had said it.

The next I heard of Simpkins he was dead. The Associated Press dispatches announced it, the Cuban Junta confirmed it, and last of all, a long dispatch from Simpkins himself detailed the circumstances leading up to the " atrocity," as the headlines in his paper called it.

I got a long wire from Ezra's father asking me to see the managing editor and get at the facts for him. It seemed that the paper had thought a heap of Simpkins, and that he had been sent out to Cuba as a correspondent, and stationed with the Insurgent army. Simpkins in Cuba had evidently lived up to the reputation of Simpkins in Chicago. When there was any news he sent it, and when there wasn't he just made news and sent that along.

The first word of his death had come in his own letter, brought across on a filibustering steamer and wired on from Jacksonville. It told, with close attention to detail— something he had learned since he left me —how he had strayed away from the little band of insurgents with which he had been out scouting and had blundered into the Spanish lines. He had been promptly made a prisoner, and, despite his papers proving his American citizenship, and the nature of his job, and the red cross on his sleeve, he had been tried by drumhead court martial and sentenced to be shot at dawn. All this he had written out, and then, that his account might be complete, he had gone on and imagined his own execution. This was written in a sort of pigeon, or perhaps you would call it black Spanish, English, and let on to be the work of the eyewitness to whom Simpkins had confided his letter. He had been the sentry over the prisoner, and for a small bribe in hand and the promise of a larger one from the paper, he had turned his back on Simpkins while he wrote out the story, and afterward had deserted and carried it to the Cuban lines.

The account ended: " Then, as the order to fire was given by the lieutenant, Señor Simpkins raised his eyes toward Heaven and cried: ' I protest in the name of my American citizenship! ' " At the end of the letter, and not intended for publication, was scrawled: " This is a bully scoop for you, boys, but it's pretty tough on me. Good-by. Simpkins."

The managing editor dashed a tear from

his eye when he read this to me, and gulped a little as he said: "I can't help it; he was such a d——d thoughtful boy. Why, he even remembered to inclose descriptions for the pictures!"

Simpkins' last story covered the whole of the front page and three columns of the second, and it just naturally sold cords of papers. His editor demanded that the State Department take it up, though the Spaniards denied the execution or any previous knowledge of any such person as this Señor Simpkins. That made another page in the paper, of course, and then they got up a memorial service, which was good for three columns. One of those fellows that you can find in every office, who goes around and makes the boys give up their lunch money to buy flowers for the deceased aunt of the cellar boss' wife, managed to collect twenty dollars among our clerks, and they sent a floral notebook, with "Gone to Press," done

108

in blue immortelles on the cover, as their "tribute."

I put on a plug hat and attended the service out of respect for his father. But I had hardly got back to the office before I received a wire from Jamaica, reading: "Cable your correspondent here let me have hundred. Notify father all hunk. Keep it dark from others. Simpkins."

I kept it dark and Ezra came back to life by easy stages and in such a way as not to attract any special attention to himself. He managed to get the impression around that he'd been snatched from the jaws of death by a rescue party at the last moment. The last I heard of him he was in New York and drawing ten thousand a year, which was more than he could have worked up to in the leather business in a century.

Fifty or a hundred years ago, when there was good money in poetry, a man with Simpkins' imagination would naturally have been a bard, as I believe they used to call the top-notchers; and, once he was turned loose to root for himself, he instinctively smelled out the business where he could use a little poetic license and made a hit in it.

When a pup has been born to point partridges there's no use trying to run a fox with him. I was a little uncertain about you at first, but I guess the Lord intended you to hunt with the pack. Get the scent in your nostrils and keep your nose to the ground, and don't worry too much about the end of the chase. The fun of the thing's in the run and not in the finish.

> Your affectionate father,
> JOHN GRAHAM.

No. 9

FROM John Graham, at Hot Springs, Arkansas, to his son, Pierrepont, at the Union Stock Yards in Chicago. Mr. Pierrepont has been investing more heavily in roses than his father thinks his means warrant, and he tries to turn his thoughts to staple groceries.

IX

Dear Pierrepont: I knew right off that I had made a mistake when I opened the inclosed and saw that it was a bill for fifty-two dollars, " for roses sent, as per orders, to Miss Mabel Dashkam." I don't just place Miss Dashkam, but if she's the daughter of old Job Dashkam, on the open Board, I should say, on general principles, that she was a fine girl to let some other fellow marry. The last time I saw her, she inventoried about $10,000 as she stood—allowing that her diamonds would scratch glass—and that's more capital than any woman has a right to tie up on her back, I don't care how rich her father is. And Job's fortune is one of that brand which foots up to a million in the newspapers and leaves the heirs in debt to the lawyers who settle the estate.

Of course I've never had any real experience in this sparking business, except with your Ma; but I've watched from the other side of the fence while a heap of fellows were getting it, and I should say that marrying a woman like Mabel Dashkam would be the first step toward becoming a grass widower. I'll bet if you'll tell her you're making twelve a week and ain't going to get any more till you earn it, you'll find that you can't push within a mile of her even on a Soo ice-breaker. She's one of those women with a heart like a stock-ticker—it doesn't beat over anything except money.

Of course you're in no position yet to think of being engaged even, and that's why I'm a little afraid that you may be planning to get married. But a twelve-dollar clerk, who owes fifty-two dollars for roses, needs a keeper more than a wife. I want to say right here that there always comes a time to the fellow who blows fifty-two dollars at a lick on roses when he thinks how many staple groceries he could have bought with the money. After all, there's no fool like a young fool, because in the nature of things he's got a long time to live.

I suppose I'm fanning the air when I ask you to be guided by my judgment in this matter, because, while a young fellow will consult his father about buying a horse, he's cock-sure of himself when it comes to picking a wife. Marriages may be made in Heaven, but most engagements are made in the back parlor with the gas so low that a fellow doesn't really get a square look at what he's taking. While a man doesn't see much of a girl's family when he's courting, he's apt to see a good deal of it when he's housekeeping; and while he doesn't marry his wife's father, there's nothing in the marriage vow to prevent the old man from borrowing money of him, and you can bet if he's old Job Dashkam he'll do it. A man can't pick his own mother, but he can pick his son's mother, and when he chooses a father-in-law who plays the bucket shops, he needn't be surprised if his own son plays the races.

Never marry a poor girl who's been raised like a rich one. She's simply traded the virtues of the poor for the vices of the rich without going long on their good points. To marry for money or to marry without money is a crime. There's no real objection to marrying a woman with a fortune, but there is to marrying a fortune with a woman. Money makes the mare go, and it makes her cut up, too, unless she's used to it and you drive her with a snaffle-bit.

While you are at it, there's nothing like picking out a good-looking wife, because even the handsomest woman looks homely sometimes, and so you get a little variety; but a homely one can only look worse than usual. Beauty is only skin deep, but that's deep enough to satisfy any reasonable man. (I want to say right here that to get any sense out of a proverb I usually find that I have to turn it wrong side out.) Then, too, if a fellow's bound to marry a fool, and a lot of men have to if they're going to hitch up into a well-matched team, there's nothing like picking a good-looking one.

I simply mention these things in a general way, because it seems to me, from the gait at which you're starting off, that you'll likely find yourself roped and branded any day, without quite knowing how it happened, and I want you to understand that the girl who marries you for my money is getting a package of green goods in more ways than one. I think, though, if you really understood what marrying on twelve a week meant, you would have bought a bed-room set instead of roses with that fifty-two you owe.

Speaking of marrying the old man's money by proxy naturally takes me back to my old town in Missouri and the case of Chauncey Witherspoon Hoskins. Chauncey's father was the whole village, barring the railroad station and the saloon, and, of course, Chauncey thought that he was something of a pup himself. So he was, but not just the kind that Chauncey thought he was. He stood about five foot three in his pumps, had a nice pinky complexion, pretty wavy hair, and a curly mustache. All he needed was a blue ribbon around his neck to make you call, " Here, Fido," when he came into the room.

Still I believe he must have been pretty popular with the ladies, because I can't think of him to this day without wanting to punch his head. At the church sociables he used to hop around among them, chipping and chirping like a dicky-bird picking up seed; and he was a great hand to play the piano, and sing saddish, sweetish songs to them. Always said the smooth thing and said it easy. Never had to choke and swallow to fetch it up. Never stepped through his partner's dress when he began to dance, or got flustered when he brought her refreshments and poured the coffee in her lap to cool instead of in the saucer. We boys who couldn't walk across the floor without feeling that our pants had hiked up till they showed our feet to the knees, and that we were carrying a couple of canvased hams where our hands ought to be, didn't like him; but the girls did. You can trust a woman's taste on everything except men; and it's mighty lucky that she slips up there or we'd pretty nigh all be bachelors. I might add that you can't trust a man's taste on women, either, and that's pretty lucky, too, because there are a good many old maids in the world as it is.

One time or another Chauncey lolled in the best room of every house in our town, and we used to wonder how he managed to browse up and down the streets that way without getting into the pound. I never found out till after I married your Ma, and she told me Chauncey's heart secrets. It really wasn't violating any confidence, because he'd told them to every girl in town.

Seems he used to get terribly sad as soon as he was left alone with a girl and began to hint about a tragedy in his past—something that had blighted his whole life and left him without the power to love again—and lots more slop from the same pail.

Of course, every girl in that town had known Chauncey since he wore short pants, and ought to have known that the nearest to a tragedy he had ever been was when he sat in the top gallery of a Chicago theatre and saw a lot of barnstormers play Othello. But some people, and especially very young people, don't think anything's worth believing unless it's hard to believe.

Chauncey worked along these lines until he was twenty-four, and then he made a mistake. Most of the girls that he had grown up with had married off, and while he was waiting for a new lot to come along, he began to shine up to the widow Sharpless, a powerful, well-preserved woman of forty or thereabouts, who had been born with her eye-teeth cut. He found her uncommon sympathetic. And when Chauncey finally came out of his trance he was the stepfather of the widow's four children.

She was very kind to Chauncey, and treated him like one of her own sons; but she was very, very firm. There was no gallivanting off alone, and when they went out in double harness strangers used to annoy him considerable by patting him on the head and saying to his wife: " What a bright-looking chap your son is, Mrs. Hoskins! "

She was almost seventy when Chauncey buried her a while back, and they say that he began to take notice again on the way home from the funeral. Anyway, he crowded his mourning into sixty days—and I reckon there was plenty of room in them to hold all his grief without stretching— and his courting into another sixty. And four months after date he presented his matrimonial papers for acceptance. Said he was tired of this mother-and-son foolishness, and wasn't going to leave any room for doubt this time. Didn't propose to have people sizing his wife up for one of his ancestors any more. So he married Lulu Littlebrown, who was just turned eighteen. Chauncey was over fifty then, and wizened up like a late pippin that has been out overnight in an early frost.

He took Lu to Chicago for the honeymoon, and Mose Greenebaum, who happened to be going up to town for his fall goods, got into the parlor car with them. By and by the porter came around and stopped beside Chauncey.

" Wouldn't your daughter like a pillow under her head? " says he.

Chauncey just groaned. Then—" Git; you Senegambian son of darkness! " And the porter just naturally got.

Mose had been taking it all in, and now he went back to the smoking-room and passed the word along to the drummers there. Every little while one of them would lounge up the aisle to Chauncey and ask if he couldn't lend his daughter a magazine, or give her an orange, or bring her a drink And the language that he gave back in return for these courtesies wasn't at all fitting in a bridegroom. Then Mose had another happy thought, and dropped off at a way station and wired the clerk at the Palmer House.

When they got to the hotel the clerk was on the lookout for them, and Chauncey hadn't more than signed his name before he reached out over his diamond and said: " Ah, Mr. Hoskins; would you like to have your daughter near you? "

I simply mention Chauncey in passing as an example of the foolishness of thinking you can take any chances with a woman who has really decided that she wants to marry, or that you can average up matrimonial mistakes. And I want you to remember that marrying the wrong girl is the one mistake that you've got to live with all your life. I think, though, that if you tell Mabel what your assets are, she'll decide she won't be your particular mistake.

Your affectionate father,

JOHN GRAHAM.

No. 10

FROM John Graham, at the Union Stock Yards in Chicago, to his son, Pierrepont, at the Commercial House, Jeffersonville, Indiana. Mr. Pierrepont has been promoted to the position of traveling salesman for the house, and has started out on the road.

X

Dear Pierrepont: When I saw you start off yesterday I was just a little uneasy; for you looked so blamed important and chesty that I am inclined to think you will tell the first customer who says he doesn't like our sausage that he knows what he can do about it. Repartee makes reading lively, but business dull. And what the house needs is more orders.

Sausage is the one subject of all others that a fellow in the packing business ought to treat solemnly. Half the people in the world take a joke seriously from the start, and the other half if you repeat it often enough. Only last week the head of our sausage department started to put out a tin-tag brand of frankfurts, but I made him take it off the market quicker than lightning, because I knew that the first fool who saw the tin-tag would ask if that was the

127

license. And, though people would grin a little at first, they'd begin to look serious after a while; and whenever the butcher tried to sell them our brand they'd imagine they heard the bark, and ask for " that real country sausage " at twice as much a pound.

He laughs best who doesn't laugh at all when he's dealing with the public. It has been my experience that, even when a man has a sense of humor, it only really carries him to the point where he will join in a laugh at the expense of the other fellow. There's nothing in the world sicker-looking than the grin of the man who's trying to join in heartily when the laugh's on him, and to pretend that he likes it.

Speaking of sausage with a registered pedigree calls to mind a little experience that I had last year. A fellow came into the office here with a shriveled-up toy spaniel, one of those curly, hairy little fellows that a woman will kiss, and then grumble because a fellow's mustache tickles.

" *You looked so blamed important and chesty when you started off.*"

Said he wanted to sell him. I wasn't really disposed to add a dog to my troubles, but on general principles I asked him what he wanted for the little cuss.

The fellow hawed and choked and wiped away a tear. Finally, he fetched out that he loved the dog like a son, and that it broke his heart to think of parting with him; that he wouldn't dare look Dandy in the face after he had named the price he was asking for him, and that it was the record-breaking, marked-down sacrifice sale of the year on dogs; that it wasn't really money he was after, but a good home for the little chap. Said that I had a rather pleasant face and he knew that he could trust me to treat Dandy kindly; so—as a gift—he would let me have him for five hundred.

" Cents? " says I.

" Dollars," says he, without blinking.

" It ought to be a mastiff at that price," says I.

" If you thought more of quality," says

he, in a tone of sort of dignified reproof, " and less of quantity, your brand would enjoy a better reputation."

I was pretty hot, I can tell you, but I had laid myself open, so I just said: " The sausage business is too poor to warrant our paying any such price for light-weights. Bring around a bigger dog and then we'll talk; " but the fellow only shook his head sadly, whistled to Dandy, and walked off.

I simply mention this l'ttle incident as an example of the fact that when a man cracks a joke in the Middle Ages he's apt to affect the sausage market in the Nineteenth Century, and to lay open an honest butcher to the jeers of every dog-stealer in the street. There's such a thing as carrying a joke too far, and the fellow who keeps on pretending to believe that he's paying for pork and getting dog is pretty apt to get dog in the end.

But all that aside, I want you to get it firmly fixed in your mind right at the start that this trip is only an experiment, and that I am not at all sure you were cut out by the Lord to be a drummer. But you can figure on one thing—that you will never become the pride of the pond by starting out to cut figure eights before you are firm on your skates.

A real salesman is one-part talk and nine-parts judgment; and he uses the nine-parts of judgment to tell when to use the one-part of talk. Goods ain't sold under Marquess of Queensberry rules any more, and you'll find that knowing how many rounds the Old 'Un can last against the Boiler-Maker won't really help you to load up the junior partner with our Corn-fed brand hams.

A good many salesmen have an idea that buyers are only interested in baseball, and funny stories, and Tom Lipton, and that business is a side line with them; but as a matter of fact mighty few men work up to the position of buyer through giving up their office hours to listening to anecdotes. I never saw one that liked a drummer's jokes more than an eighth of a cent a pound on a tierce of lard. What the house really sends you out for is orders.

Of course, you want to be nice and mellow with the trade, but always remember that mellowness carried too far becomes rottenness. You can buy some fellows with a cheap cigar and some with a cheap compliment, and there's no objection to giving a man what he likes, though I never knew smoking to do anything good except a ham, or flattery to help any one except to make a fool of himself.

Real buyers ain't interested in much besides your goods and your prices. Never run down your competitor's brand to them, and never let them run down yours. Don't get on your knees for business, but don't hold your nose so high in the air that an order can travel under it without your seeing it. You'll meet a good many people on the road that you won't like, but the house needs their business.

Some fellows will tell you that we play the hose on our dry salt meat before we ship it, and that it shrinks in transit like a Baxter Street Jew's all-wool suits in a rainstorm; that they wonder how we manage to pack solid gristle in two-pound cans without leaving a little meat hanging to it; and that the last car of lard was so strong that it came back of its own accord from every retailer they shipped it to. The first fellow will be lying, and the second will be exaggerating, and the third may be telling the truth. With him you must settle on the spot; but always remember that a man who's making a claim never underestimates his case, and that you can generally compromise for something less than the first figure. With the second you must sympathize, and say that the matter will be reported to headquarters and the boss of the canning-room

133

called up on the carpet and made to promise that it will never happen again. With the first you needn't bother. There's no use feeding expensive "hen-food" to an old Dominick that sucks eggs. The chances are that the car weighed out more than it was billed, and that the fellow played the hose on it himself and added a thousand pounds of cheap salt before he jobbed it out to his trade.

Where you're going to slip up at first is in knowing which is which, but if you don't learn pretty quick you'll not travel very far for the house. For your own satisfaction I will say right here that you may know you are in a fair way of becoming a good drummer by three things:

First—When you send us Orders.

Second—More Orders.

Third—Big Orders.

If you do this you won't have a great deal of time to write long letters, and we won't have a great deal of time to read them, for we will be very, very busy here making and shipping the goods. We aren't specially interested in orders that the other fellow gets, or in knowing how it happened after it has happened. If you like life on the road you simply won't let it happen. So just send us your address every day and your orders. They will tell us all that we want to know about "the situation."

I was cured of sending information to the house when I was very, very young—in fact, on the first trip which I made on the road. I was traveling out of Chicago for Hammer & Hawkins, wholesale dry-goods, gents' furnishings and notions. They started me out to round up trade in the river towns down Egypt ways, near Cairo.

I hadn't more than made my first town and sized up the population before I began to feel happy, because I saw that business ought to be very good there. It appeared as if everybody in that town needed something in my line. The clerk of the hotel where I registered wore a dicky and his cuffs were tied to his neck by pieces of string run up his sleeves, and most of the merchants on Main Street were in their shirt-sleeves—at least those that had shirts were—and so far as I could judge there wasn't a whole pair of galluses among them. Some were using wire, some a little rope, and others just faith —buckled extra tight. Pride of the Prairie XXX flour sacks seemed to be the nobby thing in boys' suitings there. Take it by and large, if ever there was a town which looked as if it had a big, short line of dry-goods, gents' furnishings and notions to cover, it was that one.

But when I caught the proprietor of the general store during a lull in the demand for navy plug, he wouldn't even look at my samples, and when I began to hint that the people were pretty ornery dressers he reckoned that he " would paste me one if I warn't so young." Wanted to know what I meant by coming swelling around in song-

and-dance clothes and getting funny at the expense of people who made their living honestly. Allowed that when it came to a humorous get-up my clothes were the original end-man's gag.

I noticed on the way back to the hotel that every fellow holding up a hitching-post was laughing, and I began to look up and down the street for the joke, not understanding at first that the reason why I couldn't see it was because I was it. Right there I began to learn that, while the Prince of Wales may wear the correct thing in hats, it's safer when you're out of his sphere of influence to follow the styles that the hotel clerk sets; that the place to sell clothes is in the city, where every one seems to have plenty of them; and that the place to sell mess pork is in the country, where every one keeps hogs. That is why when a fellow comes to me for advice about moving to a new country, where there are more opportunities, I advise him—if he is built right

—to go to an old city where there is more money.

I wrote in to the house pretty often on that trip, explaining how it was, going over the whole situation very carefully, and telling what our competitors were doing, wherever I could find that they were doing anything.

I gave old Hammer credit for more curiosity than he possessed, because when I reached Cairo I found a telegram from him reading: *"Know what our competitors are doing: they are getting all the trade. But what are you doing?"* I saw then that the time for explaining was gone and that the moment for resigning had arrived; so I just naturally sent in my resignation. That is what we will expect from you—or orders.

Your affectionate father,

JOHN GRAHAM.

No. 11

FROM John Graham, at the Union Stock Yards in Chicago, to his son, Pierrepont, at The Planters' Palace Hotel, at Big Gap, Kentucky. Mr. Pierrepont's orders are small and his expenses are large, so his father feels pessimistic over his prospects.

XI

Dear Pierrepont: You ought to be feeling mighty thankful to-day to the fellow who invented fractions, because while your selling cost for last month was within the limit, it took a good deal of help from the decimal system to get it there. You are in the position of the boy who was chased by the bull— open to congratulations because he reached the tree first, and to condolence because a fellow up a tree, in the middle of a forty-acre lot, with a disappointed bull for company, is in a mighty bad fix.

I don't want to bear down hard on you right at the beginning of your life on the road, but I would feel a good deal happier over your showing if you would make a downright failure or a clean-cut success once in a while, instead of always just skinning through this way. It looks to me as if you were trying only half as hard as

you could, and in trying it's the second half
that brings results. If there's one piece of
knowledge that is of less use to a fellow
than knowing when he's beat, it's knowing
when he's done just enough work to keep
from being fired. Of course, you are bright
enough to be a half-way man, and to hold a
half-way place on a half-way salary by
doing half the work you are capable of, but
you've got to add dynamite and ginger and
jounce to your equipment if you want to get
the other half that's coming to you. You've
got to believe that the Lord made the first
hog with the Graham brand burned in the
skin, and that the drove which rushed down
a steep place was packed by a competitor.
You've got to know your goods from A to
Izzard, from snout to tail, on the hoof and
in the can. You've got to know 'em like a
young mother knows baby talk, and to be
as proud of 'em as the young father of a
twelve-pound boy, without really thinking
that you're stretching it four pounds.

You've got to believe in yourself and make your buyers take stock in you at par and accrued interest. You've got to have the scent of a bloodhound for an order, and the grip of a bulldog on a customer. You've got to feel the same personal solicitude over a bill of goods that strays off to a competitor as a parson over a backslider, and hold special services to brin͜ it back into the fold. You've got to get p every morning with determination if you're going to go to bed with satisfaction. You've got to eat hog, think hog, dream hog—in short, go the whole hog if you're going to win out in the pork-packing business.

That's a pretty liberal receipt, I know, but it's intended for a fellow who wants to make a good-sized pie. And the only thing you ever find in pastry that you don't put in yourself is flies.

You have had a wide-open chance during the last few months to pick up a good deal about the practical end of the business, and between trips now you ought to spend every spare minute in the packing-house getting posted. Nothing earns better interest than judicious questions, and the man who invests in more knowledge of the business than he has to have in order to hold his job has capital with which to buy a mortgage on a better one.

I may be mistaken, but I am just a little afraid that you really did not get beyond a bowing acquaintance with Mr. Porker when you were here at the packing-house. Of course, there isn't anything particularly pretty about a hog, but any animal which has its kindly disposition and benevolent inclination to yield up a handsome margin of profit to those who get close to it, is worthy of a good deal of respect and attention.

I ain't one of those who believe that a half knowledge of a subject is useless, but it has been my experience that when a fellow has that half knowledge he finds it's the

144

other half which would really come in handy. So, when a man's in the selling end of the business what he really needs to know is the manufacturing end; and when he's in the factory he can't know too much about the trade.

You're just about due now to run into a smart Aleck buyer who'll show you a sample of lard which he'll say was made by a competitor, and ask what you think the grand jury ought to do to a house which had the nerve to label it "leaf." Of course, you will nose around it and look wise and say that, while you hesitate to criticize, you are afraid it would smell like a hot-box on a freight if any one tried to fry doughnuts in it. That is the place where the buyer will call for Jack and Charlie to get in on the laugh, and when he has wiped away the tears he will tell you that it is your own lard, and prove it to you. Of course, there won't be anything really the matter with it, and if you had been properly posted you would have looked surprised when he showed it to you and have said:

"I don't quite diagnose the case your way, Mr. Smith; that's a blamed sight better lard than I thought Muggins & Co. were making." And you'd have driven a spike right through that fellow's little joke and have nailed down his order hard and tight with the same blow.

What you know is a club for yourself, and what you don't know is a meat-ax for the other fellow. That is why you want to be on the lookout all the time for information about the business, and to nail a fact just as a sensible man nails a mosquito— the first time it settles near him. Of course, a fellow may get another chance, but the odds are that if he misses the first opening he will lose a good deal of blood before he gets the second.

Speaking of finishing up a subject as you go along naturally calls to mind the case of Josh Jenkinson, back in my home town.

"Josh Jenkinson would eat a little food now and then just to be sociable, but what he really lived on was tobacco."

As I first remember Josh, he was just bone and by-products. Wasn't an ounce of real meat on him. In fact, he was so blamed thin that when he bought an outfit of clothes his wife used to make them over into two suits for him. Josh would eat a little food now and then, just to be sociable, but what he really lived on was tobacco. Usually kept a chew in one cheek and a cob pipe in the other. He was a powerful hand for a joke and had one of those porous heads and movable scalps which go with a sense of humor in a small village. Used to scare us boys by drawing in on his pipe and letting the smoke sort of leak out through his eyes and ears and nose. Pretended that he was the devil and that he was on fire inside. Old Doc Hoover caught him at it once and told us that he wasn't, but allowed that he was a blood relation.

Elder Hoover was a Methodist off the tip of the sirloin. There weren't any evasions or generalities or metaphors in his religion.

The lower layers of the hereafter weren't Hades or Gehenna with him, but just plain Hell, and mighty hot, too, you bet. His creed was built of sheet iron and bolted together with inch rivets. He kept the fire going under the boiler night and day, and he was so blamed busy stoking it that he didn't have much time to map out the golden streets. When he blew off it was superheated steam and you could see the sinners who were in range fairly sizzle and parboil and shrivel up. There was no give in Doc; no compromises with creditors; no fire sales. He wasn't one of those elders who would let a fellow dance the lancers if he'd swear off on waltzing; or tell him it was all right to play whist in the parlor if he'd give up penny-ante at the Dutchman's; or wink at his smoking if he'd quit whisky.

Josh knew this, so he kept away from the camp-meeting, though the Elder gunned for him pretty steady for a matter of five years. But one summer when the meetings

148

were extra interesting, it got so lonesome
sitting around with the whole town off in
the woods that Josh sneaked out to the edge
of the camp and hid behind some bushes
where he could hear what was going on.
The elder was carrying about two hundred
and fifty pounds, by the gauge, that day,
and with that pressure he naturally traveled
into the sinners pretty fast. The first thing
Josh knew he was out from under cover and
a-hallelujahing down between the seats to
the mourners' bench. When the elder saw
what was coming he turned on the forced
draft. Inside of ten minutes he had Josh
under conviction and had taken his pipe
and plug away from him.

I am just a little inclined to think that
Josh would have backslid if he hadn't been
a practical joker, and a critter of that breed
is about as afraid of a laugh on himself as
a raw colt of a steam roller. So he stuck it
out, and began to take an interest in meal
time. Kicked because it didn't come eight

or ten times a day. The first thing he knew he had fatted up till he filled out his half suit and had to put it away in camphor. Then he bought a whole suit, living-skeleton size. In two weeks he had strained a shoulder seam and looked as if he was wearing tights. So he retired it from circulation and moved up a size. That one was a little loose, and it took him a good month to crowd it.

Josh was a pretty hefty man now, but he kept right on bulging out, building on an addition here and putting out a bay window there, all the time retiring new suits, until his wife had fourteen of them laid away in the chest.

Said it didn't worry him; that he was bound to lose flesh sooner or later. That he would catch them on the way down, and wear them out one at a time. But when he got up to three hundred and fifty pounds he just stuck. Tried exercise and dieting and foreign waters, but he couldn't budge an ounce. In the end he had to give the clothes to the Widow Doolan, who had fourteen sons in assorted sizes.

I simply mention Josh in passing as an example of the fact that a fellow can't bank on getting a chance to go back and take up a thing that he has passed over once, and to call your attention to the fact that a man who knows his own business thoroughly will find an opportunity sooner or later of reaching the most hardened cuss of a buyer on his route and of getting a share of his.

I want to caution you right here against learning all there is to know about pork-packing too quick. Business is a good deal like a nigger's wool—it doesn't look very deep, but there are a heap of kinks and curves in it.

When I was a boy and the fellow in pink tights came into the ring, I used to think he was doing all that could be reasonably expected when he kept eight or ten glass balls going in the air at once. But the

151

beautiful lady in the blue tights would keep right on handing him things—kerosene lamps and carving knives and miscellaneous cutlery and crockery, and he would get them going, too, without losing his happy smile. The great trouble with most young fellows is that they think they have learned all they need to know and have given the audience its money's worth when they can keep the glass balls going, and so they balk at the kerosene lamps and the rest of the implements of light housekeeping. But there's no real limit to the amount of extras a fellow with the right stuff in him will take on without losing his grin.

I want to see you come up smiling; I want to feel you in the business, not only on pay day but every other day. I want to know that you are running yourself full time and overtime, stocking up your brain so that when the demand comes you will have the goods to offer. So far, you promise to make a fair to ordinary salesman among our retail trade. I want to see you grow into a car-lot man—so strong and big that you will force us to see that you are out of place among the little fellows. Buck up!

Your affectionate father,

JOHN GRAHAM.

No. 12

FROM John Graham, at the Union Stock Yards in Chicago, to his son, Pierrepont, at Little Delmonico's, Prairie Centre, I n d i a n a. Mr. Pierrepont has annoyed his father by accepting his criticisms in a spirit of gentle, but most reprehensible, resignation.

XII

Dear Pierrepont: Don't ever write me another of those sad, sweet, gentle sufferer letters. It's only natural that a colt should kick a trifle when he's first hitched up to the break wagon, and I'm always a little suspicious of a critter that stands too quiet under the whip. I know it's not meekness, but meanness, that I've got to fight, and it's hard to tell which is the worst.

The only animal which the Bible calls patient is an ass, and that's both good doctrine and good natural history. For I had to make considerable of a study of the Missouri mule when I was a boy, and I discovered that he's not really patient, but that he only pretends to be. You can cuss him out till you've nothing but holy thoughts left in you to draw on, and you can lay the rawhide on him till he's striped like a circus zebra, and if you're cautious and reserved in his company he will just look grieved and pained and resigned. But all the time that mule will be getting meaner and meaner inside, adding compound cussedness every thirty days, and practicing drop kicks in his stall after dark.

Of course, nothing in this world is wholly bad, not even a mule, for he is half horse. But my observation has taught me that the horse half of him is the front half, and that the only really safe way to drive him is hind-side first. I suppose that you could train one to travel that way, but it really doesn't seem worth while when good roadsters are so cheap.

That's the way I feel about these young fellows who lazy along trying to turn in at every gate where there seems to be a little shade, and sulking and balking whenever you say " git-ap " to them. They are the men who are always howling that Bill Smith was promoted because he had a pull, and that they are being held down because the manager is jealous of them. I've seen a good many pulls in my time, but I never saw one strong enough to lift a man any higher than he could raise himself by his boot straps, or long enough to reach through the cashier's window for more money than its owner earned.

When a fellow brags that he has a pull, he's a liar or his employer's a fool. And when a fellow whines that he's being held down, the truth is, as a general thing, that his boss can't hold him up. He just picks a nice, soft spot, stretches out flat on his back, and yells that some heartless brute has knocked him down and is sitting on his chest.

A good man is as full of bounce as a cat with a small boy and a bull terrier after him. When he's thrown to the dog from the second-story window, he fixes while he's sailing through the air to land right, and when the dog jumps for the spot where he hits, he isn't there, but in the top of the tree across the street. He's a good deal like the little red-headed cuss that we saw in the football game you took me to. Every time the herd stampeded it would start in to trample and paw and gore him. One minute the whole bunch would be on top of him and the next he would be loping off down the range, spitting out hair and pieces of canvas jacket, or standing on one side as cool as a hog on ice, watching the mess unsnarl and the removal of the cripples.

I didn't understand football, but I understood that little sawed-off. He knew his business. And when a fellow knows his business, he doesn't have to explain to people that he does. It isn't what a man knows, but what he thinks he knows that he brags about. Big talk means little knowledge.

There's a vast difference between having a carload of miscellaneous facts sloshing around loose in your head and getting all mixed up in transit, and carrying the same assortment properly boxed and crated for convenient handling and immediate delivery. A ham never weighs so much as when it's half cured. When it has soaked in all the pickle that it can, it has to sweat out most of it in the smoke-house before it is any real good; and when you've soaked up all the information you can hold, you will have to forget half of it before you will be of any real use to the house. If there's anything worse than knowing too little, it's knowing too much. Education will broaden a narrow mind, but there's no known cure for a big head. The best you can hope is that it will swell up and bust; and then, of course, there's nothing left. Poverty never spoils a good man, but prosperity often does. It's easy to stand hard times, because that's the only thing you can do, but in good times the fool-killer has to do night work.

I simply mention these things in a general way. A good many of them don't apply to you, no doubt, but it won't do any harm to make sure. Most men get cross-eyed when they come to size themselves up, and see an angel instead of what they're trying to look at. There's nothing that tells the truth to a woman like a mirror, or that lies harder to a man.

What I am sure of is that you have got the sulks too quick. If you knew all that you'll have to learn before you'll be a big, broad-gauged merchant, you might have something to be sulky about.

When you've posted yourself properly about the business you'll have taken a step in the right direction—you will be able to get your buyer's attention. All the other steps are those which lead you into his confidence.

Right here you will discover that you are in the fix of the young fellow who married his best girl and took her home to live with his mother. He found that the only way in which he could make one happy was by making the other mad, and that when he tried to make them both happy he only succeeded in making them both mad. Naturally, in the end, his wife divorced him and his mother disinherited him, and left her money to an orphan asylum, because, as she sensibly observed in the codicil, "orphans can not be ungrateful to their parents." But if the man had had a little tact he would have kept them in separate houses, and have let each one think that she was getting a trifle the best of it, without really giving it to either.

Tact is the knack of keeping quiet at the right time; of being so agreeable yourself that no one can be disagreeable to you; of making inferiority feel like equality. A tactful man can pull the stinger from a bee without getting stung.

Some men deal in facts, and call Bill Jones a liar. They get knocked down. Some men deal in subterfuges, and say that Bill Jones' father was a kettle-rendered liar, and that his mother's maiden name was Sapphira, and that any one who believes in the Darwinian theory should pity rather than blame their son. They get disliked. But your tactful man says that since Baron Munchausen no one has been so chuck full of bully reminiscences as Bill Jones; and when that comes back to Bill he is half tickled 'to death, because he doesn't know that the higher criticism has hurt the Baron's reputation. That man gets the trade.

There are two kinds of information: one to which everybody's entitled, and that is taught at school; and one which nobody ought to know except yourself, and that is what you think of Bill Jones. Of course, where you feel a man is not square you will be armed to meet him, but never on his own ground. Make him be honest with you if you can, but don't let him make you dishonest with him.

When you make a mistake, don't make the second one—keeping it to yourself. Own up. The time to sort out rotten eggs is at the nest. The deeper you hide them in the case the longer they stay in circulation, and the worse impression they make when they finally come to the breakfast-table. A mistake sprouts a lie when you cover it up. And one lie breeds enough distrust to choke out the prettiest crop of confidence that a fellow ever cultivated.

Of course, it's easy to have the confidence of the house, or the confidence of the buyer, but you've got to have both. The house pays you your salary, and the buyer helps you earn it. If you skin the buyer you will lose your trade; and if you play tag with the house you will lose your job. You've simply got to walk the fence straight, for if you step to either side you'll find a good deal of air under you.

Even after you are able to command the attention and the confidence of your buyers, you've got to be up and dressed all day to hold what trade is yours, and twisting and turning all night to wriggle into some of the other fellow's. When business is good, that is the time to force it, because it will come easy; and when it is bad, that is the time to force it, too, because we will need the orders.

Speaking of making trade naturally calls to my mind my old acquaintance, Herr Doctor Paracelsus Von Munsterberg, who, when I was a boy, came to our town " fresh from his healing triumphs at the Courts of Europe," as his handbills ran, " not to make money, but to confer on suffering mankind the priceless boon of health; to make the sick well, and the well better."

Munsterberg wasn't one of your common, coarse, county-fair barkers. He was a pretty high-toned article. Had nice, curly black hair and didn't spare the bear's grease. Wore a silk hat and a Prince Albert coat all the time, except when he was orating, and then he shed the coat to get freer action with his arms. And when he talked he used the whole language, you bet.

" Herr Doctor Paracelsus Von Mun-
sterberg was a pretty high-toned article."

Of course, the Priceless Boon was put up in bottles, labeled Munsterberg's Miraculous Medical Discovery, and, simply to introduce it, he was willing to sell the small size at fifty cents and the large one at a dollar. In addition to being a philanthropist the Doctor was quite a hand at card tricks, played the banjo, sung coon songs and imitated a saw going through a board very creditably. All these accomplishments, and the story of how he cured the Emperor of Austria's sister with a single bottle, drew a crowd, but they didn't sell a drop of the Discovery. Nobody in town was really sick, and those who thought they were had stocked up the week before with Quackenboss' Quick Quinine Kure from a fellow that made just as liberal promises as Munsterberg and sold the large size at fifty cents, including a handsome reproduction of an old master for the parlor.

Some fellows would just have cussed a little and have moved on to the next town, but Munsterberg made a beautiful speech, praising the climate, and saying that in his humble capacity he had been privileged to meet the strength and beauty of many Courts, but never had he been in any place where strength was stronger or beauty beautifuller than right here in Hoskins' Corners. He prayed with all his heart, though it was almost too much to hope, that the cholera, which was raging in Kentucky, would pass this Eden by; that the yellow fever, which was devastating Tennessee, would halt abashed before this stronghold of health, though he felt bound to add that it was a peculiarly malignant and persistent disease; that the smallpox, which was creeping southward from Canada, would smite the next town instead of ours, though he must own that it was no respecter of persons; that the diphtheria and scarlet-fever, which were sweeping over New England and crowding the graveyards, could be kept from crossing the Hudson, though they were

168

great travelers and it was well to be prepared for the worst; that we one and all might providentially escape chills, headaches, coated tongue, pains in the back, loss of sleep and that tired feeling, but it was almost too much to ask, even of such a generous climate. In any event, he begged us to beware of worthless nostrums and base imitations. It made him sad to think that to-day we were here and that to-morrow we were running up an undertaker's bill, all for the lack of a small bottle of Medicine's greatest gift to Man.

I could see that this speech made a lot of women in the crowd powerful uneasy, and I heard the Widow Judkins say that she was afraid it was going to be " a mighty sickly winter," and she didn't know as it would do any harm to have some of that stuff in the house. But the Doctor didn't offer the Priceless Boon for sale again. He went right from his speech into an imitation of a dog, with a tin can tied to his tail, running down Main Street and crawling under Si Hooper's store at the far end of it—an imitation, he told us, to which the Sultan was powerful partial, " him being a cruel man and delighting in torturing the poor dumb beasts which the Lord has given us to love, honor and cherish."

He kept this sort of thing up till he judged it was our bedtime, and then he thanked us " one and all for our kind attention," and said that as his mission in life was to amuse as well as to heal, he would stay over till the next afternoon and give a special matinée for the little ones, whom he loved for the sake of his own golden-haired Willie, back there over the Rhine.

Naturally, all the women and children turned out the next afternoon, though the men had to be at work in the fields and the stores, and the Doctor just made us roar for half an hour. Then, while he was singing an uncommon funny song, Mrs. Brown's Johnny let out a howl.

The Doctor stopped short. " Bring the poor little sufferer here, Madam, and let me see if I can soothe his agony," says he.

Mrs. Brown was a good deal embarrassed and more scared, but she pushed Johnny, yelling all the time, up to the Doctor, who began tapping him on the back and looking down his throat. Naturally, this made Johnny cry all the harder, and his mother was beginning to explain that she " reckoned she must have stepped on his sore toe," when the Doctor struck his forehead, cried " Eureka! ", whipped out a bottle of the Priceless Boon, and forced a spoonful of it into Johnny's mouth. Then he gave the boy three slaps on the back and three taps on the stomach, ran one hand along his windpipe, and took a small button-hook out of his mouth with the other.

Johnny made all his previous attempts at yelling sound like an imitation when he saw this, and he broke away and ran toward home. Then the Doctor stuck one hand in over the top of his vest, waved the button-hook in the other, and cried: "Woman, your child is cured! Your button-hook is found!"

Then he went on to explain that when baby swallowed safety-pins, or pennies, or fish-bones, or button-hooks, or any little household articles, that all you had to do was to give it a spoonful of the Priceless Boon, tap it gently fore and aft, hold your hand under its mouth, and the little article would drop out like chocolate from a slot machine.

Every one was talking at once, now, and nobody had any time for Mrs. Brown, who was trying to say something. Finally she got mad and followed Johnny home. Half an hour later the Doctor drove out of the Corners, leaving his stock of the Priceless Boon distributed—for the usual considera-tion—among all the mothers in town.

It was not until the next day that Mrs. Brown got a chance to explain that while the Boon might be all that the Doctor claimed for it, no one in her house had ever owned a button-hook, because her old man wore jack-boots and she wore congress shoes, and little Johnny wore just plain feet.

I simply mention the Doctor in passing, not as an example in morals, but in methods. Some salesmen think that selling is like eating—to satisfy an existing appetite; but a good salesman is like a good cook—he can create an appetite when the buyer isn't hungry.

I don't care how good old methods are, new ones are better, even if they're only just as good. That's not so Irish as it sounds. Doing the same thing in the same way year after year is like eating a quail a day for thirty days. Along toward the middle of the month a fellow begins to long for a broiled crow or a slice of cold dog.

Your affectionate father,

JOHN GRAHAM.

No, 13

FROM John Graham, at the Union Stock Yards in Chicago, to his son, Pierrepont, care of The Hoosier Grocery Co., Indianapolis, Indiana. Mr. Pierrepont's orders have been looking up, so the old man gives him a pat on the back — but not too hard a one.

XIII

Dear Pierrepont: That order for a car-load of Spotless Snow Leaf from old Shorter is the kind of back talk I like. We can stand a little more of the same sort of sass-ing. I have told the cashier that you will draw thirty a week after this, and I want you to have a nice suit of clothes made and send the bill to the old man. Get something that won't keep people guessing whether you follow the horses or do buck and wing dancing for a living. Your taste in clothes seems to be lasting longer than the rest of your college education. You looked like a young widow who had raised the second crop of daisies over the deceased when you were in here last week.

Of course, clothes don't make the man, but they make all of him except his hands and face during business hours, and that's a pretty considerable area of the human ani-

177

mal. A dirty shirt may hide a pure heart, but it seldom covers a clean skin. If you look as if you had slept in your clothes, most men will jump to the conclusion that you have, and you will never get to know them well enough to explain that your head is so full of noble thoughts that you haven't time to bother with the dandruff on your shoulders. And if you wear blue and white striped pants and a red necktie, you will find it difficult to get close enough to a deacon to be invited to say grace at his table, even if you never play for anything except coffee or beans.

Appearances are deceitful, I know, but so long as they are, there's nothing like having them deceive for us instead of against us. I've seen a ten-cent shave and a five-cent shine get a thousand-dollar job, and a cigarette and a pint of champagne knock the bottom out of a million-dollar pork corner. Four or five years ago little Jim Jackson had the bears in the provision pit hibernating and living on their own fat till one morning, the day after he had run the price of mess pork up to twenty dollars and nailed it there, some one saw him drinking a small bottle just before he went on 'Change, and told it round among the brokers on the floor. The bears thought Jim must have had bad news, to be bracing up at that time in the morning, so they perked up and everlastingly sold the mess pork market down through the bottom of the pit to solid earth. There wasn't even a grease spot left of that corner when they got through. As it happened, Jim hadn't had any bad news; he just took the drink because he felt pretty good, and things were coming his way.

But it isn't enough to be all right in this world; you've got to look all right as well, because two-thirds of success is making people think you are all right. So you have to be governed by general rules, even though you may be an exception. People have seen four and four make eight, and the young man and the small bottle make a damned fool so often that they are hard to convince that the combination can work out any other way. The Lord only allows so much fun for every man that He makes. Some get it going fishing most of the time and making money the rest; some get it making money most of the time and going fishing the rest. You can take your choice, but the two lines of business don't gee. The more money, the less fish. The farther you go, the straighter you've got to walk.

I used to get a heap of solid comfort out of chewing tobacco. Picked up the habit in Missouri, and took to it like a Yankee to pie. At that time pretty much every one in those parts chewed, except the Elder and the women, and most of them snuffed. Seemed a nice, sociable habit, and I never thought anything special about it till I came North and your Ma began to tell me it was a vile relic of barbarism, meaning Missouri, I suppose. Then I confined operations to my office and took to fine cut instead of plug, as being tonier.

Well, one day, about ten years ago, when I was walking through the office, I noticed one of the boys on the mailing-desk, a mighty likely-looking youngster, sort of working his jaws as he wrote. I didn't stop to think, but somehow I was mad in a minute. Still, I didn't say a word—just stood and looked at him while he speeded up the way the boys will when they think the old man is nosing around to see whose salary he can raise next.

I stood over him for a matter of five minutes, and all the time he was pretending not to see me at all. I will say that he was a pretty game boy, for he never weakened for a second. But at last, seeing he was about to choke to death, I said, sharp and sudden—" Spit."

Well, sir, I thought it was a cloudburst. You can bet I was pretty hot, and I started in to curl up that young fellow to a crisp.

But before I got out a word, something hit me all of a sudden, and I just went up to the boy and put my hand on his shoulder and said, " Let's swear off, son."

Naturally, he swore off—he was so blamed scared that he would have quit breathing if I had asked him to, I reckon. And I had to take my stock of fine cut and send it to the heathen.

I simply mention this little incident in passing as an example of the fact that a man can't do what he pleases in this world, because the higher he climbs the plainer people can see him. Naturally, as the old man's son, you have a lot of fellows watching you and betting that you are no good. If you succeed they will say it was an accident; and if you fail they will say it was a cinch.

There are two unpardonable sins in this world—success and failure. Those who succeed can't forgive a fellow for being a failure, and those who fail can't forgive him for being a success. If you do succeed, though, you will be too busy to bother very much about what the failures think.

I dwell a little on this matter of appearances because so few men are really thinking animals. Where one fellow reads a stranger's character in his face, a hundred read it in his get-up. We have shown a dozen breeds of dukes and droves of college presidents and doctors of divinity through the packing-house, and the workmen never noticed them except to throw livers at them when they got in their way. But when John L. Sullivan went through the stock yards it just simply shut down the plant. The men quit the benches with a yell and lined up to cheer him. You see, John looked his job, and you didn't have to explain to the men that he was the real thing in prize-fighters. Of course, when a fellow gets to the point where he is something in particular, he doesn't have to care because he doesn't look like anything special; but while a young fellow isn't anything in particular, it is a mighty valuable asset if he looks like something special.

Just here I want to say that while it's all right for the other fellow to be influenced by appearances, it's all wrong for you to go on them. Back up good looks by good character yourself, and make sure that the other fellow does the same. A suspicious man makes trouble for himself, but a cautious one saves it. Because there ain't any rotten apples in the top layer, it ain't always safe to bet that the whole barrel is sound.

A man doesn't snap up a horse just because he looks all right. As a usual thing that only makes him wonder what really is the matter that the other fellow wants to sell. So he leads the nag out into the middle of a ten-acre lot, where the light will strike him good and strong, and examines every hair of his hide, as if he expected to find it near-seal, or some other base imita-

*" When John L. Sullivan
went through the stock yards,
it just simply shut down the
plant."*

tion; and he squints under each hoof for the grand hailing sign of distress; and he peeks down his throat for dark secrets. If the horse passes this degree the buyer drives him twenty or thirty miles, expecting him to turn out a roarer, or to find that he balks, or shies, or goes lame, or develops some other horse nonsense. If after all that there are no bad symptoms, he offers fifty less than the price asked, on general principles, and for fear he has missed something.

Take men and horses, by and large, and they run pretty much the same. There's nothing like trying a man in harness a while before you bind yourself to travel very far with him.

I remember giving a nice-looking, clean-shaven fellow a job on the billing-desk, just on his looks, but he turned out such a poor hand at figures that I had to fire him at the end of a week. It seemed that the morning he struck me for the place he had pawned his razor for fifteen cents in order to get a shave. Naturally, if I had known that in the first place I wouldn't have hired him as a human arithmetic.

Another time I had a collector that I set a heap of store by. Always handled himself just right when he talked to you and kept himself looking right up to the mark. His salary wasn't very big, but he had such a persuasive way that he seemed to get a dollar and a half's worth of value out of every dollar that he earned. Never crowded the fashions and never gave 'em any slack. If sashes were the thing with summer shirts, why Charlie had a sash, you bet, and when tight trousers were the nobby trick in pants, Charlie wore his double reefed. Take him fore and aft, Charlie looked all right and talked all right—always careful, always considerate, always polite.

One noon, after he had been with me for a year or two, I met him coming in from his route looking glum; so I handed him fifty dollars as a little sweetener. I never saw a fifty cheer a man up like that one did Charlie, and he thanked me just right— didn't stutter and didn't slop over. I ear-marked Charlie for a raise and a better job right there.

Just after that I got mixed up with some work in my private office and I didn't look around again till on toward closing time. Then, right outside my door I met the office manager, and he looked mighty glum, too.

" I was just going to knock on your door," said he.

" Well? " I asked.

" Charlie Chasenberry is eight hundred dollars short in his collections."

" Um—m," I said, without blinking, but I had a gone feeling just the same.

" I had a plain-clothes man here to arrest him this evening, but he didn't come in."

" Looks as if he'd skipped, eh? " I asked.

" I'm afraid so, but I don't know how. He didn't have a dollar this morning, be-cause he tried to overdraw his salary account and I wouldn't let him, and he didn't collect any bills to-day because he had already collected everything that was due this week and lost it bucking the tiger."

I didn't say anything, but I suspected that there was a sucker somewhere in the office. The next day I was sure of it, for I got a telegram from the always polite and thoughtful Charlie, dated at Montreal:

" Many, many thanks, dear Mr. Graham, for your timely assistance."

Careful as usual, you see, about the little things, for there were just ten words in the message. But that " Many, many thanks, dear Mr. Graham," was the closest to slopping over I had ever known him to come.

I consider the little lesson that Charlie gave me as cheap at eight hundred and fifty dollars, and I pass it along to you because it may save you a thousand or two on your experience account.

Your affectionate father,
JOHN GRAHAM.

No. 14

FROM John Graham, at the Union Stock Yards in Chicago, to his son, Pierrepont, at The Travelers' Rest, New Albany, Indiana. Mr. Pierrepont has taken a little flyer in short ribs on 'Change, and has accidentally come into the line of his father's vision.

XIV

Dear Pierrepont: I met young Horshey, of Horshey & Horter, the grain and provision brokers, at luncheon yesterday, and while we were talking over the light run of hogs your name came up somehow, and he congratulated me on having such a smart son. Like an old fool, I allowed that you were bright enough to come in out of the rain if somebody called you, though I ought to have known better, for it seems as if I never start in to brag about your being sound and sweet that I don't have to wind up by allowing a rebate for skippers.

Horshey was so blamed anxious to show that you were over-weight—he wants to handle some of my business on 'Change—that he managed to prove you a light-weight. Told me you had ordered him to sell a hundred thousand ribs short last week, and that he had just bought them in on a wire from you at a profit of four hundred and sixty-odd dollars. I was mighty hot, you bet, to know that you had been speculating, but I had to swallow and allow that you were a pretty sharp boy. I told Horshey to close out the account and send me a check for your profits and I would forward it, as I wanted to give you a tip on the market before you did any more trading.

I inclose the check herewith. Please indorse it over to the treasurer of The Home for Half Orphans and return at once. I will see that he gets it with your compliments.

Now, I want to give you that tip on the market. There are several reasons why it isn't safe for you to trade on 'Change just now, but the particular one is that Graham & Co. will fire you if you do. Trading on margin is a good deal like paddling around the edge of the old swimming hole—it seems safe and easy at first, but before a fellow knows it he has stepped off the edge into deep water. The wheat pit is only thirty feet across, but it reaches clear down to Hell. And trading on margin means trading on the ragged edge of nothing. When a man buys, he's buying something that the other fellow hasn't got. When a man sells, he's selling something that he hasn't got. And it's been my experience that the net profit on nothing is nit. When a speculator wins he don't stop till he loses, and when he loses he can't stop till he wins.

You have been in the packing business long enough now to know that it takes a bull only thirty seconds to lose his hide; and if you'll believe me when I tell you that they can skin a bear just as quick on 'Change, you won't have a Board of Trade Indian using your pelt for a rug during the long winter months.

Because you are the son of a pork packer you may think that you know a little more than the next fellow about paper pork. There's nothing in it. The poorest men on earth are the relations of millionaires.

When I sell futures on 'Change, they're against hogs that are traveling into dry salt at the rate of one a second, and if the market goes up on me I've got the solid meat to deliver. But, if you lose, the only part of the hog which you can deliver is the squeal.

I wouldn't bear down so hard on this matter if money was the only thing that a fellow could lose on 'Change. But if a clerk sells pork, and the market goes down, he's mighty apt to get a lot of ideas with holes in them and bad habits as the small change of his profits. And if the market goes up, he's likely to go short his self-respect to win back his money.

Most men think that they can figure up all their assets in dollars and cents, but a merchant may owe a hundred thousand dollars and be solvent. A man's got to lose more than money to be broke. When a fellow's got a straight backbone and a clear eye his creditors don't have to lie awake nights worrying over his liabilities. You can hide your meanness from your brain and your tongue, but the eye and the backbone won't keep secrets. When the tongue lies, the eyes tell the truth.

I know you'll think that the old man is bucking and kicking up a lot of dust over a harmless little flyer. But I've kept a heap smarter boys than you out of Joliet when they found it easy to feed the Board of Trade hog out of my cash drawer, after it had sucked up their savings in a couple of laps.

You must learn not to overwork a dollar any more than you would a horse. Three per cent. is a small load for it to draw; six, a safe one; when it pulls in ten for you it's likely working out West and you've got to watch to see that it doesn't buck; when it makes twenty you own a blame good critter or a mighty foolish one, and you want to make dead sure which; but if it draws a hundred it's playing the races or something just as hard on horses and dollars, and the first thing you know you won't have even a carcass to haul to the glue factory.

I dwell a little on this matter of speculation because you've got to live next door to the Board of Trade all your life, and it's a safe thing to know something about a neighbor's dogs before you try to pat them. Sure Things, Straight Tips and Dead Cinches will come running out to meet you, wagging their tails and looking as innocent as if they hadn't just killed a lamb, but they'll bite. The only safe road to follow in speculation leads straight away from the Board of Trade on the dead run.

Speaking of sure things naturally calls to mind the case of my old friend Deacon Wiggleford, whom I used to know back in Missouri years ago. The Deacon was a powerful pious man, and he was good according to his lights, but he didn't use a very superior article of kerosene to keep them burning.

Used to take up half the time in prayer-

meeting talking about how we were all weak
vessels and stewards. But he was so blamed
busy exhorting others to give out of the full-
ness with which the Lord had blessed them
that he sort of forgot that the Lord had
blessed him about fifty thousand dollars'
worth, and put it all in mighty safe property, too, you bet.

The Deacon had a brother in Chicago
whom he used to call a sore trial. Brother
Bill was a broker on the Board of Trade,
and, according to the Deacon, he was not
only engaged in a mighty sinful occupation,
but he was a mighty poor steward of his sinful gains. Smoked two-bit cigars and wore
a plug hat. Drank a little and cussed a
little and went to the Episcopal Church,
though he had been raised a Methodist. Altogether it looked as if Bill was a pretty
hard nut.

Well, one fall the Deacon decided to go to
Chicago himself to buy his winter goods, and
naturally he hiked out to Brother Bill's to

stay, which was considerable cheaper for him than the Palmer House, though, as he told us when he got back, it made him sick to see the waste.

The Deacon had his mouth all fixed to tell Brother Bill that, in his opinion, he wasn't much better than a faro dealer, for he used to brag that he never let anything turn him from his duty, which meant his meddling in other people's business. I want to say right here that with most men duty means something unpleasant which the other fellow ought to do. As a matter of fact, a man's first duty is to mind his own business. It's been my experience that it takes about all the thought and work which one man can give to run one man right, and if a fellow's putting in five or six hours a day on his neighbor's character, he's mighty apt to scamp the building of his own.

Well, when Brother Bill got home from business that first night, the Deacon explained that every time he lit a two-bit cigar

he was depriving a Zulu of twenty-five helpful little tracts which might have made a
better man of him; that fast horses were a
snare and plug hats a wile of the Enemy;
that the Board of Trade was the Temple
of Belial and the brokers on it his sons and
servants.

Brother Bill listened mighty patiently to
him, and when the Deacon had pumped out
all the Scripture that was in him, and was
beginning to suck air, he sort of slunk into
the conversation like a setter pup that's
been caught with the feathers on its chops.

"Brother Zeke," says he, "I shall certainly let your words soak in. I want to be
a number two red, hard, sound and clean
sort of a man, and grade contract on delivery day. Perhaps, as you say, the rust
has got into me and the Inspector won't
pass me, and if I can see it that way I'll
settle my trades and get out of the market
for good."

The Deacon knew that Brother Bill had

scraped together considerable property, and, as he was a bachelor, it would come to him in case the broker was removed by any sudden dispensation. What he really feared was that this money might be fooled away in high living and speculation. And so he had banged away into the middle of the flock, hoping to bring down those two birds. Now that it began to look as if he might kill off the whole bunch he started in to hedge.

"Is it safe, William?" says he.

"As Sunday-school," says Bill, "if you do a strictly brokerage business and don't speculate."

"I trust, William, that you recognize the responsibilities of your stewardship?"

Bill fetched a groan. "Zeke," says he, "you cornered me there, and I 'spose I might as well walk up to the Captain's office and settle. I hadn't bought or sold a bushel on my own account in a year till last week, when I got your letter saying that you were coming. Then I saw what looked like a

" *I started in to curl up*
that young fellow to a crisp."

safe chance to scalp the market for a couple of cents a bushel, and I bought 10,000 September, intending to turn over the profits to you as a little present, so that you could see the town and have a good time without it's costing you anything."

The Deacon judged from Bill's expression that he had got nipped and was going to try to unload the loss on him, so he changed his face to the one which he used when attending the funeral of any one who hadn't been a professor, and came back quick and hard:

" I'm surprised, William, that you should think I would accept money made in gambling. Let this be a lesson to you. How much did you lose? "

" That's the worst of it—I didn't lose; I made two hundred dollars," and Bill hove another sigh.

" Made two hundred dollars! " echoed the Deacon, and he changed his face again for the one which he used when he found a lead quarter in his till and couldn't remember who had passed it on him.

"Yes," Bill went on, "and I'm ashamed of it, for you've made me see things in a new light. Of course, after what you've said, I know it would be an insult to offer you the money. And I feel now that it wouldn't be right to keep it myself. I must sleep on it and try to find the straight thing to do."

I guess it really didn't interfere with Bill's sleep, but the Deacon sat up with the corpse of that two hundred dollars, you bet. In the morning at breakfast he asked Brother Bill to explain all about this speculating business, what made the market go up and down, and whether real corn or wheat or pork figured in any stage of a deal. Bill looked sort of sad and dreamy-eyed, as if his conscience hadn't digested that two hundred yet, but he was mighty obliging about explaining everything to Zeke. He had changed his face for the one which he wore when he sold an easy customer ground peas and chicory for O. G. Java, and every now and then he gulped as if he was going to start a hymn. When Bill told him how good and bad weather sent the market up and down, he nodded and said that that part of it was all right, because the weather was of the Lord.

" Not on the Board of Trade it isn't," Bill answered back; " at least, not to any marked extent; it's from the weather man or some liar in the corn belt, and, as the weather man usually guesses wrong, I reckon there isn't any special inspiration about it. The game is to guess what's going to happen, not what has happened, and by the time the real weather comes along everybody has guessed wrong and knocked the market off a cent or two."

That made the Deacon's chin whiskers droop a little, but he began to ask questions again, and by and by he discovered that away behind—about a hundred miles behind, but that was close enough for the Deacon—a deal in futures there were real wheat and pork. Said then that he'd been misinformed and misled; that speculation was a legitimate business, involving skill and sagacity; that his last scruple was removed, and that he would accept the two hundred.

Bill brightened right up at that and thanked him for putting it so clear and removing the doubts that had been worrying him. Said that he could speculate with a clear conscience after listening to the Deacon's able exposition of the subject. Was only sorry he hadn't seen him to talk it over before breakfast, as the two hundred had been lying so heavy on his mind all night that he'd got up early and mailed a check for it to the Deacon's pastor and told him to spend it on his poor.

Zeke took the evening train home in order to pry that check out of the elder, but old Doc. Hoover was a pretty quick stepper himself and he'd blown the whole two hundred as soon as he got it, buying winter coal for poor people.

I simply mention the Deacon in passing as an example of the fact that it's easy for a man who thinks he's all right to go all wrong when he sees a couple of hundred dollars lying around loose a little to one side of the straight and narrow path; and that when he reaches down to pick up the money there's usually a string tied to it and a small boy in the bushes to give it a yank. Easy-come money never draws interest; easy-borrowed dollars pay usury.

Of course, the Board of Trade and every other commercial exchange have their legitimate uses, but all you need to know just now is that speculation by a fellow who never owns more pork at a time than he sees on his breakfast plate isn't one of them. When you become a packer you may go on 'Change as a trader; until then you can go there only as a sucker.

Your affectionate father,

JOHN GRAHAM.

No. 15

FROM John Graham, at the Union Stock Yards in Chicago, to his son, Pierrepont, at The Scrub Oaks, Spring Lake, Michigan. Mr. Pierrepont has been promoted again, and the old man sends him a little advice with his appointment.

XV

Dear Pierrepont: I judge from yours of
the twenty-ninth that you must have the
black bass in those parts pretty well ter-
rorized. I never could quite figure it out,
but there seems to be something about a fish
that makes even a cold-water deacon see
double. I reckon it must be that while Eve
was learning the first principles of dress-
making from the snake, Adam was off bass
fishing and keeping his end up by learning
how to lie.

Don't overstock yourself with those four-
pound fish yarns, though, because the boys
have been bringing them back from their
vacations till we've got enough to last us for
a year of Fridays. And if you're sending
them to keep in practice, you might as well
quit, because we've decided to take you off
the road when you come back, and make
you assistant manager of the lard depart-

ment. The salary will be fifty dollars a week, and the duties of the position to do your work so well that the manager can't run the department without you, and that you can run the department without the manager.

To do this you will have to know lard; to know yourself; and to know those under you. To some fellows lard is just hog fat, and not always that, if they would rather make a dollar to-day than five to-morrow. But it was a good deal more to Jack Summers, who held your new job until we had to promote him to canned goods.

Jack knew lard from the hog to the frying pan; was up on lard in history and religion; originated what he called the " Ham and " theory, proving that Moses' injunction against pork must have been dissolved by the Circuit Court, because Noah included a couple of shoats in his cargo, and called one of his sons Ham, out of gratitude, prob- ably, after tasting a slice broiled for the first time; argued that all the great nations lived on fried food, and that America was the greatest of them all, owing to the energy-producing qualities of pie, liberally shortened with lard.

It almost broke Jack's heart when we decided to manufacture our new cottonseed oil product, Seedoiline. But on reflection he saw that it just gave him an extra hold on the heathen that he couldn't convert to lard, and he started right out for the Hebrew and vegetarian vote. Jack had enthusiasm, and enthusiasm is the best shortening for any job; it makes heavy work light.

A good many young fellows envy their boss because they think he makes the rules and can do as he pleases. As a matter of fact, he's the only man in the shop who can't. He's like the fellow on the tight-rope— there's plenty of scenery under him and lots of room around him, but he's got to keep his feet on the wire all the time and travel straight ahead.

A clerk has just one boss to answer to—the manager. But the manager has just as many bosses as he has clerks under him. He can make rules, but he's the only man who can't afford to break them now and then. A fellow is a boss simply because he's a better man than those under him, and there's a heap of responsibility in being better than the next fellow.

No man can ask more than he gives. A fellow who can't take orders can't give them. If his rules are too hard for him to mind, you can bet they are too hard for the clerks who don't get half so much for minding them as he does. There's no alarm clock for the sleepy man like an early rising manager; and there's nothing breeds work in an office like a busy boss.

Of course, setting a good example is just a small part of a manager's duties. It's not enough to settle yourself firm on the box seat—you must have every man under you hitched up right and well in hand. You can't work individuals by general rules. Every man is a special case and needs a special pill.

When you fix up a snug little nest for a Plymouth Rock hen and encourage her with a nice porcelain egg, it doesn't always follow that she has reached the fricassee age because she doesn't lay right off. Sometimes she will respond to a little red pepper in her food.

I don't mean by this that you ever want to drive your men, because the lash always leaves its worst soreness under the skin. A hundred men will forgive a blow in the face where one will a blow to his self-esteem. Tell a man the truth about himself and shame the devil if you want to, but you won't shame the man you're trying to reach, because he won't believe you. But if you can start him on the road that will lead him to the truth he's mighty apt to try to reform himself before any one else finds him out.

Consider carefully before you say a hard

word to a man, but never let a chance to say a good one go by. Praise judiciously bestowed is money invested.

Never learn anything about your men except from themselves. A good manager needs no detectives, and the fellow who can't read human nature can't manage it. The phonograph records of a fellow's character are lined in his face, and a man's days tell the secrets of his nights.

Be slow to hire and quick to fire. The time to discover incompatibility of temper and curl-papers is before the marriage ceremony. But when you find that you've hired the wrong man, you can't get rid of him too quick. Pay him an extra month, but don't let him stay another day. A discharged clerk in the office is like a splinter in the thumb—a centre of soreness. There are no exceptions to this rule, because there are no exceptions to human nature.

Never threaten, because a threat is a promise to pay that it isn't always convenient to meet, but if you don't make it good it hurts your credit. Save a threat till you're ready to act, and then you won't need it. In all your dealings, remember that to-day is your opportunity; to-morrow some other fellow's.

Keep close to your men. When a fellow's sitting on top of a mountain he's in a mighty dignified and exalted position, but if he's gazing at the clouds, he's missing a heap of interesting and important doings down in the valley. Never lose your dignity, of course, but tie it up in all the red tape you can find around the office, and tuck it away in the safe. It's easy for a boss to awe his clerks, but a man who is feared to his face is hated behind his back. A competent boss can move among his men without having to draw an imaginary line between them, because they will see the real one if it exists.

Besides keeping in touch with your office men, you want to feel your salesmen all the time. Send each of them a letter every day so that they won't forget that we are making goods for which we need orders; and insist on their sending you a line every day, whether they have anything to say or not. When a fellow has to write in six times a week to the house, he uses up his explanations mighty fast, and he's pretty apt to hustle for business to make his seventh letter interesting.

Right here I want to repeat that in keeping track of others and their faults it's very, very important that you shouldn't lose sight of your own. Authority swells up some fellows so that they can't see their corns; but a wise man tries to cure his own while remembering not to tread on his neighbors'.

In this connection, the story of Lemuel Hostitter, who kept the corner grocery in my old town, naturally comes to mind. Lem was probably the meanest white man in the State of Missouri, and it wasn't any walk-over to hold the belt in those days.

"*A good many salesmen have an idea that buyers are only interested in funny stories.*"

Most grocers were satisfied to adulterate their coffee with ground peas, but Lem was so blamed mean that he adulterated the peas first. Bought skin-bruised hams and claimed that the bruise was his private and particular brand, stamped in the skin, showing that they were a fancy article, packed expressly for his fancy family trade. Ran a soda-water fountain in the front of his store with home-made syrups that ate the lining out of the children's stomachs, and a blind tiger in the back room with moonshine whiskey that pickled their daddies' insides. Take it by and large, Lem's character smelled about as various as his store, and that wasn't perfumed with lily-of-the-valley, you bet.

One time and another most men dropped into Lem's store of an evening, because there wasn't any other place to go and swap lies about the crops and any of the neighbors who didn't happen to be there. As Lem was always around, in the end he was the only man in town whose meanness hadn't been talked over in that grocery. Naturally, he began to think that he was the only decent white man in the county. Got to shaking his head and reckoning that the town was plum rotten. Said that such goings on would make a pessimist of a goat. Wanted to know if public opinion couldn't be aroused so that decency would have a show in the village.

Most men get information when they ask for it, and in the end Lem fetched public opinion all right. One night the local chapter of the W. C. T. U. borrowed all the loose hatchets in town and made a good, clean, workmanlike job of the back part of his store, though his whiskey was so mean that even the ground couldn't soak it up. The noise brought out the men, and they sort of caught the spirit of the happy occasion. When they were through, Lem's stock and fixtures looked mighty sick, and they had Lem on a rail headed for the county line.

I don't know when I've seen a more surprised man than Lem. He couldn't cuss even. But as he never came back, to ask for any explanation, I reckon he figured it out that they wanted to get rid of him because he was too good for the town.

I simply mention Lem in passing as an example of the fact that when you're through sizing up the other fellow, it's a good thing to step back from yourself and see how you look. Then add fifty per cent. to your estimate of your neighbor for virtues that you can't see, and deduct fifty per cent. from yourself for faults that you've missed in your inventory, and you'll have a pretty accurate result.

Your affectionate father,
JOHN GRAHAM.

No. 16

FROM John Graham, at the Schweitzer-kasenhof, Karlsbad, Austria, to his son, Pierrepont, at the Union Stock Yards, Chicago. Mr. Pierrepont has shown mild symptoms of an attack of society fever, and his father is administering some simple remedies.

XVI

Dear Pierrepont: If you happen to run across Doc Titherington you'd better tell him to go into training, because I expect to be strong enough to lick him by the time I get back. Between that ten-day boat which he recommended and these Dutch doctors, I'm almost well and about broke. You don't really have to take the baths here to get rid of your rheumatism—their bills scare it out of a fellow.

They tell me we had a pretty quiet trip across, and I'm not saying that we didn't, because for the first three days I was so busy holding myself in my berth that I couldn't get a chance to look out the port-hole to see for myself. I reckon there isn't anything alive that can beat me at being seasick, unless it's a camel, and he's got three stomachs.

When I did get around I was a good deal

223

of a maverick—for all the old fellows were playing poker in the smoking-room and all the young ones were lallygagging under the boats—until I found that we were carrying a couple of hundred steers between decks. They looked mighty homesick, you bet, and I reckon they sort of sized me up as being a long ways from Chicago, for we cottoned to each other right from the start. Take 'em as they ran, they were a mighty likely bunch of steers, and I got a heap of solid comfort out of them. There must have been good money in them, too, for they reached England in prime condition.

I wish you would tell our people at the Beef House to look into this export cattle business, and have all the facts and figures ready for me when I get back. There seems to be a good margin in it, and with our English house we are fixed up to handle it all right at this end. It makes me mighty sick to think that we've been sitting back on our hindlegs and letting the other fellow run away with this trade. We are packers, I know, but that's no reason why we can't be shippers, too. I want to milk the critter coming and going, twice a day, and milk her dry. Unless you do the whole thing you can't do anything in business as it runs to-day. There's still plenty of room at the top, but there isn't much anywheres else.

There may be reasons why we haven't been able to tackle this exporting of live cattle, but you can tell our people there that they have got to be mighty good reasons to wipe out the profit I see in it. Of course, I may have missed them, for I've only looked into the business a little by way of recreation, but it won't do to say that it's not in our line, because anything which carries a profit on four legs is in our line.

I dwell a little on the matter because, while this special case is out of your department, the general principle is in it. The way to think of a thing in business is to think of it first, and the way to get a share of the trade is to go for all of it. Half the battle's in being on the hilltop first; and the other half's in staying there. In speaking of these matters, and in writing you about your new job, I've run a little ahead of your present position, because I'm counting on you to catch up with me. But you want to get it clearly in mind that I'm writing to you not as the head of the house, but as the head of the family, and that I don't propose to mix the two things.

Even as assistant manager of the lard department, you don't occupy a very important position with us yet. But the great trouble with some fellows is that a little success goes to their heads. Instead of hiding their authority behind their backs and trying to get close to their men, they use it as a club to keep them off. And a boss with a case of big-head will fill an office full of sore heads.

I don't know any one who has better opportunities for making himself unpopular than an assistant, for the clerks are apt to cuss him for all the manager's meanness, and the manager is likely to find fault with him for all the clerks' cussedness. But if he explains his orders to the clerks he loses his authority, and if he excuses himself to the manager he loses his usefulness. A manager needs an assistant to take trouble from him, not to bring it to him.

The one important thing for you to remember all the time is not to forget. It's easier for a boss to do a thing himself than to tell some one twice to do it. Petty details take up just as much room in a manager's head as big ideas; and the more of the first you store for him, the more warehouse room you leave him for the second. When a boss has to spend his days swearing at his assistant and the clerks have to sit up nights hating him, they haven't much time left to swear by the house. Satisfaction is the oil of the business machine.

Some fellows can only see those above

them, and others can only see those under them, but a good man is cross-eyed and can see both ends at once. An assistant who becomes his manager's right hand is going to find the left hand helping him; and it's not hard for a clerk to find good points in a boss who finds good ones in him. Pulling from above and boosting from below make climbing easy.

In handling men, your own feelings are the only ones that are of no importance. I don't mean by this that you want to sacrifice your self-respect, but you must keep in mind that the bigger the position the broader the man must be to fill it. And a diet of courtesy and consideration gives girth to a boss.

Of course, all this is going to take so much time and thought that you won't have a very wide margin left for golf—especially in the afternoons. I simply mention this in passing, because I see in the Chicago papers which have been sent me that you

228

were among the players on the links one afternoon a fortnight ago. Golf's a nice, foolish game, and there ain't any harm in it so far as I know except for the balls—the stiff balls at the beginning, the lost balls in the middle, and the highballs at the end of the game. But a young fellow who wants to be a boss butcher hasn't much daylight to waste on any kind of links except sausage links.

Of course, a man should have a certain amount of play, just as a boy is entitled to a piece of pie at the end of his dinner, but he don't want to make a meal of it. Any one who lets sinkers take the place of bread and meat gets bilious pretty young; and these fellows who haven't any job, except to blow the old man's dollars, are a good deal like the little niggers in the pie-eating contest at the County Fair—they've a-plenty of pastry and they're attracting a heap of attention, but they've got a stomach-ache coming to them by and by.

I want to caution you right here against getting the society bug in your head. I'd sooner you'd smoke these Turkish cigarettes which smell like a fire in the fertilizer factory. You're going to meet a good many stray fools in the course of business every day without going out to hunt up the main herd after dark.

Everybody over here in Europe thinks that we haven't any society in America, and a power of people in New York think that we haven't any society in Chicago. But so far as I can see there are just as many ninety-nine-cent men spending million-dollar incomes in one place as another; and the rules that govern the game seem to be the same in all three places—you've got to be a descendant to belong, and the farther you descend the harder you belong. The only difference is that, in Europe, the ancestor who made money enough so that his family could descend, has been dead so long that they have forgotten his shop; in New York he's so recent that they can only pretend to have forgotten it; but in Chicago they can't lose it because the ancestor is hustling on the Board of Trade or out at the Stock Yards. I want to say right here that I don't propose to be an ancestor until after I'm dead. Then, if you want to have some fellow whose grandfather sold bad whiskey to the Indians sniff and smell pork when you come into the room, you can suit yourself.

Of course, I may be off in sizing this thing up, because it's a little out of my line. But it's been my experience that these people who think that they are all the choice cuts off the critter, and that the rest of us are only fit for sausage, are usually chuck steak when you get them under the knife. I've tried two or three of them, who had gone broke, in the office, but when you separate them from their money there's nothing left, not even their friends.

I never see a fellow trying to crawl or to buy his way into society that I don't think of my old friend Hank Smith and his wife Kate—Kate Botts she was before he married her—and how they tried to butt their way through the upper crust.

Hank and I were boys together in Missouri, and he stayed along in the old town after I left. I heard of him on and off as tending store a little, and farming a little, and loafing a good deal. Then I forgot all about him, until one day a few years ago when he turned up in the papers as Captain Henry Smith, the Klondike Gold King, just back from Circle City, with a million in dust and anything you please in claims. There's never any limit to what a miner may be worth in those, except his imagination.

I was a little puzzled when, a week later, my office boy brought me a card reading Colonel Henry Augustus Bottes-Smythe, but I supposed it was some distinguished foreigner who had come to size me up so that he could round out his roast on Chi-

cago in his new book, and I told the boy to
show the General in.

I've got a pretty good memory for faces,
and I'd bought too much store plug of Hank
in my time not to know him, even with a
clean shave and a plug hat. Some men dry
up with success, but it was just spouting out
of Hank. Told me he'd made his pile and
that he was tired of living on the slag heap;
that he'd spent his whole life where money
hardly whispered, let alone talked, and he
was going now where it would shout.
Wanted to know what was the use of being
a nob if a fellow wasn't the nobbiest sort of
a nob. Said he'd bought a house on Beacon
Hill, in Boston, and that if I'd prick up my
ears occasionally I'd hear something drop
into the Back Bay. Handed me his new
card four times and explained that it was
the rawest sort of dog to carry a brace of
names in your card holster; that it gave you
the drop on the swells every time, and that

233

they just had to throw up both hands and pass you the pot when you showed down. Said that Bottes was old English for Botts, and that Smythe was new American for Smith; the Augustus was just a fancy touch, a sort of high-card kicker.

I didn't explain to Hank, because it was congratulations and not explanations that he wanted, and I make it a point to show a customer the line of goods that he's looking for. And I never heard the full particulars of his experiences in the East, though, from what I learned afterward, Hank struck Boston with a bang, all right.

He located his claim on Beacon Hill, between a Mayflower descendant and a Declaration Signer's great-grandson, breeds which believe that when the Lord made them He was through, and that the rest of us just happened. And he hadn't been in town two hours before he started in to make improvements. There was a high wrought-iron railing in front of his house, and he had that

234

gilded first thing, because, as he said, he wasn't running a receiving vault and he didn't want any mistakes. Then he bought a nice, open barouche, had the wheels painted red, hired a nigger coachman and started out in style to be sociable and get acquainted. Left his card all the way down one side of Beacon Street, and then drove back leaving it on the other. Everywhere he stopped he found that the whole family was out. Kept it up a week, on and off, but didn't seem to have any luck. Thought that the men must be hot sports and the women great gadders to keep on the jump so much. Allowed that they were the liveliest little lot of fleas that he had ever chased. Decided to quit trying to nail 'em one at a time, and planned out something that he reckoned would round up the whole bunch.

Hank sent out a thousand invitations to his grand opening, as he called it; left one at every house within a mile. Had a brass band on the front steps and fireworks on the roof. Ordered forty kegs from the brewery and hired a fancy mixer to sling together mild snorts, as he called them, for the ladies. They tell me that, when the band got to going good on the steps and the fireworks on the roof, even Beacon Street looked out the windows to see what was doing. There must have been ten thousand people in the street and not a soul but Hank and his wife and the mixer in the house. Some one yelled speech, and then the whole crowd took it up, till Hank came out on the steps. He shut off the band with one hand and stopped the fireworks with the other. Said that speechmaking wasn't his strangle-hold; that he'd been living on snowballs in the Klondike for so long that his gas-pipe was frozen; but that this welcome started the ice and he thought about three fingers of the plumber's favorite prescription would cut out the frost. Would the crowd join him? He had invited a few friends in for

236

the evening, but there seemed to be some misunderstanding about the date, and he hated to have good stuff curdle on his hands.

While this was going on, the Mayflower descendant was telephoning for the police from one side and the Signer's great-grandson from the other, and just as the crowd yelled and broke for the house two patrol wagons full of policemen got there. But they had to turn in a riot call and bring out the reserves before they could break up Hank's little Boston tea-party.

After all, Hank did what he started out to do with his party—rounded up all his neighbors in a bunch, though not exactly according to schedule. For next morning there were so many descendants and great-grandsons in the police court to prefer charges that it looked like a reunion of the Pilgrim Fathers. The Judge fined Hank on sixteen counts and bound him over to keep the peace for a hundred years. That afternoon he left for the West on a special, because the Limited didn't get there quick enough. But before going he tacked on the front door of his house a sign which read:

> " Neighbors paying their party calls will please not heave rocks through windows to attract attention. Not in and not going to be. Gone back to Circle City for a little quiet.
>
> " Yours truly,
> " HANK SMITH.

> " N. B.—Too swift for your uncle."

Hank dropped by my office for a minute on his way to 'Frisco. Said he liked things lively, but there was altogether too much rough-house on Beacon Hill for him. Judged that as the crowd which wasn't invited was so blamed sociable, the one which was invited would have stayed a week if it hadn't slipped up on the date. That might be the Boston idea, but he wanted a little more refinement in his. Said he was a pretty free spender, and would hold his end up, but he hated a hog. Of course I told Hank that Boston wasn't all that it was cracked up to be in the school histories, and that Circle City wasn't so tough as it read in the newspapers, for there was no way of making him understand that he might have lived in Boston for a hundred years without being invited to a strawberry sociable. Because a fellow cuts ice on the Arctic Circle, it doesn't follow that he's going to be worth beans on the Back Bay.

I simply mention Hank in a general way. His case may be a little different, but it isn't any more extreme than lots of others all around you over there and me over here. Of course, I want you to enjoy good society, but any society is good society where congenial men and women meet together for wholesome amusement. But I want you to keep away from people who choose play for a profession. A man's as good as he makes himself, but no man's any good because his grandfather was.

Your affectionate father,

JOHN GRAHAM.

No. 17

FROM John Graham, at the London House of Graham & Co., to his son, Pierrepont, at the Union Stock Yards in Chicago. Mr. Pierrepont has written his father that he is getting along famously in his new place.

XVII

Dear Pierrepont: Well, I'm headed for home at last, checked high and as full of prance as a spotted circus horse. Those Dutchmen ain't so bad as their language, after all, for they've fixed up my rheumatism so that I can bear down on my right leg without thinking that it's going to break off.

I'm glad to learn from your letter that you're getting along so well in your new place, and I hope that when I get home your boss will back up all the good things which you say about yourself. For the future, however, you needn't bother to keep me posted along this line. It's the one subject on which most men are perfectly frank, and it's about the only one on which it isn't necessary to be. There's never any use trying to hide the fact that you're a jim-dandy —you're bound to be found out. Of course, you want to have your eyes open all the time for a good man, but follow the old maid's example—look under the bed and in the closet, not in the mirror, for him. A man who does big things is too busy to talk about them. When the jaws really need exercise, chew gum.

Some men go through life on the Sarsaparilla Theory—that they've got to give a hundred doses of talk about themselves for every dollar which they take in; and that's a pretty good theory when you're getting a dollar for ten cents' worth of ingredients. But a man who's giving a dollar's worth of himself for ninety-nine cents doesn't need to throw in any explanations.

Of course, you're going to meet fellows right along who pass as good men for a while, because they say they're good men; just as a lot of fives are in circulation which are accepted at their face value until they work up to the receiving teller. And you're going to see these men taking buzzards and coining eagles from them that will fool

244

people so long as they can keep them in the air; but sooner or later they're bound to swoop back to their dead horse, and you'll get the buzzard smell.

Hot air can take up a balloon a long ways, but it can't keep it there. And when a fellow's turning flip-flops up among the clouds, he's naturally going to have the farmers gaping at him. But in the end there always comes a time when the parachute fails to work. I don't know anything that's quite so dead as a man who's fallen three or four thousand feet off the edge of a cloud.

The only way to gratify a taste for scenery is to climb a mountain. You don't get up so quick, but you don't come down so sudden. Even then, there's a chance that a fellow may slip and fall over a precipice, but not unless he's foolish enough to try short-cuts over slippery places; though some men can manage to fall down the hall stairs and break their necks. The path isn't the shortest way to the top, but it's usually the safest way.

Life isn't a spurt, but a long, steady climb. You can't run far up-hill without stopping to sit down. Some men do a day's work and then spend six lolling around admiring it. They rush at a thing with a whoop and use up all their wind in that. And when they're rested and have got it back, they whoop again and start off in a new direction. They mistake intention for determination, and after they have told you what they propose to do and get right up to doing it, they simply peter out.

I've heard a good deal in my time about the foolishness of hens, but when it comes to right-down, plum foolishness, give me a rooster, every time. He's always strutting and stretching and crowing and bragging about things with which he had nothing to do. When the sun rises, you'd think that he was making all the light, instead of all the noise; when the farmer's wife throws the scraps in the henyard, he crows as if he was the provider for the whole farmyard and was asking a blessing on the food; when he meets another rooster, he crows; and when the other rooster licks him, he crows; and so he keeps it up straight through the day. He even wakes up during the night and crows a little on general principles. But when you hear from a hen, she's laid an egg, and she don't make a great deal of noise about it, either.

I speak of these things in a general way, because I want you to keep in mind all the time that steady, quiet, persistent, plain work can't be imitated or replaced by anything just as good, and because your request for a job for Courtland Warrington naturally brings them up. You write that Court says that a man who has occupied his position in the world naturally can't cheapen himself by stepping down into any little piddling job where he'd have to do undignified things.

247

I want to start right out by saying that I know Court and his whole breed like a glue factory, and that we can't use him in our business. He's one of those fellows who start in at the top and naturally work down to the bottom, because that is where they belong. His father gave him an interest in the concern when he left college, and since the old man failed three years ago and took a salary himself, Court's been sponging on him and waiting for a nice, dignified job to come along and steal him. But we are not in the kidnapping business.

The only undignified job I know of is loafing, and nothing can cheapen a man who sponges instead of hunting any sort of work, because he's as cheap already as they can be made. I never could quite understand these fellows who keep down every decent instinct in order to keep up appearance, and who will stoop to any sort of real meanness to boost up their false pride.

They always remind me of little Fatty

" *Jim Hicks dared Fatty Wilkins
to eat a piece of dirt.*"

Wilkins, who came to live in our town back in Missouri when I was a boy. His mother thought a heap of Fatty, and Fatty thought a heap of himself, or his stomach, which was the same thing. Looked like he'd been taken from a joke book. Used to be a great eater. Stuffed himself till his hide was stretched as tight as a sausage skin, and then howled for painkiller. Spent all his pennies for cakes, because candy wasn't filling enough. Hogged 'em in the shop, for fear he would have to give some one a bite if he ate them on the street.

The other boys didn't take to Fatty, and they didn't make any special secret of it when he was around. He was a mighty brave boy and a mighty strong boy and a mighty proud boy—with his mouth; but he always managed to slip out of anything that looked like a fight by having a sore hand or a case of the mumps. The truth of the matter was that he was afraid of every-thing except food, and that was the thing which was hurting him most. It's mighty seldom that a fellow's afraid of what he ought to be afraid of in this world.

Of course, like most cowards, while Fatty always had an excuse for not doing something that might hurt his skin, he would take a dare to do anything that would hurt his self-respect, for fear the boys would laugh at him, or say that he was afraid, if he refused. So one day during recess Jim Hicks dared him to eat a piece of dirt. Fatty hesitated a little, because, while he was pretty promiscuous about what he put into his stomach, he had never included dirt in his bill-of-fare. But when the boys began to say that he was afraid, Fatty up and swallowed it.

And when he dared the other boys to do the same thing and none of them would take the dare, it made him mighty proud and puffed up. Got to charging the bigger boys and the loungers around the post-office a cent to see him eat a piece of dirt the size of a hickory-nut. Found there was good money in that, and added grasshoppers, at two cents apiece, as a side line. Found them so popular that he took on chinch bugs at a nickel, and fairly coined money. The last I heard of Fatty he was in a Dime Museum, drawing two salaries—one as " The Fat Man," and the other as " Launcelot, The Locust Eater, the Only Man Alive with a Gizzard."

You are going to meet a heap of Fatties, first and last, fellows who'll eat a little dirt " for fun " or to show off, and who'll eat a little more because they find that there's some easy money or times in it. It's hard to get at these men, because when they've lost everything they had to be proud of, they still keep their pride. You can always bet that when a fellow's pride makes him touchy, it's because there are some mighty raw spots on it.

It's been my experience that pride is usually a spur to the strong and a drag on the weak. It drives the strong man along and holds the weak one back. It makes the fellow with the stiff upper lip and the square jaw smile at a laugh and laugh at a sneer; it keeps his conscience straight and his back humped over his work; it makes him appreciate the little things and fight for the big ones. But it makes the fellow with the retreating forehead do the thing that looks right, instead of the thing that is right; it makes him fear a laugh and shrivel up at a sneer; it makes him live to-day on to-morrow's salary; it makes him a cheap imitation of some Willie who has a little more money than he has, without giving him zip enough to go out and force luck for himself.

I never see one of these fellows swelling around with their petty larceny pride that I don't think of a little experience of mine when I was a boy. An old fellow caught me lifting a watermelon in his patch, one afternoon, and instead of cuffing me and letting

252

me go, as I had expected if I got caught, he led me home by the ear to my ma, and told her what I had been up to.

Your grandma had been raised on the old-fashioned plan, and she had never heard of these new-fangled theories of reasoning gently with a child till its under lip begins to stick out and its eyes to fill with tears as it sees the error of its ways. She fetched the tears all right, but she did it with a trunk strap or a slipper. And your grandma was a pretty substantial woman. Nothing of the tootsey-wootsey about her foot, and nothing of the airy-fairy trifle about her slipper. When she was through I knew that I'd been licked—polished right off to a point—and then she sent me to my room and told me not to poke my nose out of it till I could recite the Ten Commandments and the Sunday-school lesson by heart.

There was a whole chapter of it, and an Old Testament chapter at that, but I laid right into it because I knew ma, and supper was only two hours off. I can repeat that chapter still, forward and backward, without missing a word or stopping to catch my breath.

Every now and then old Doc Hoover used to come into the Sunday-school room and scare the scholars into fits by going around from class to class and asking questions. That next Sunday, for the first time, I was glad to see him happen in, and I didn't try to escape attention when he worked around to our class. For ten minutes I'd been busting for him to ask me to recite a verse of the lesson, and, when he did, I simply cut loose and recited the whole chapter and threw in the Ten Commandments for good measure. It sort of dazed the Doc, because he had come to me for information about the Old Testament before, and we'd never got much beyond, And Ahab begat Jahab, or words to that effect. But when he got over the shock he made me stand right up before the whole school and do it again. Patted me on the head and said I was " an honor to my parents and an example to my playmates."

I had been looking down all the time, feeling mighty proud and scared, but at that I couldn't help glancing up to see the other boys admire me. But the first person my eye lit on was your grandma, standing in the back of the room, where she had stopped for a moment on her way up to church, and glaring at me in a mighty unpleasant way.

" Tell 'em, John," she said right out loud, before everybody.

There was no way to run, for the Elder had hold of my hand, and there was no place to hide, though I reckon I could have crawled into a rat hole. So, to gain time, I blurted out:

" Tell 'em what, mam? "

" Tell' em how you come to have your lesson so nice."

I learned to hate notoriety right then and there, but I knew there was no switching her off on to the weather when she wanted to talk religion. So I shut my eyes and let it come, though it caught on my palate once or twice on the way out.

"Hooked a watermelon, mam."

There wasn't any need for further particulars with that crowd, and they simply howled. Ma led me up to our pew, allowing that she'd tend to me Monday for disgracing her in public that way—and she did.

That was a twelve-grain dose, without any sugar coat, but it sweat more cant and false pride out of my system than I could get back into it for the next twenty years. I learned right there how to be humble, which is a heap more important than knowing how to be proud. There are mighty few men that need any lessons in that.

Your affectionate father,
JOHN GRAHAM.

No. 18

FROM John Graham, at the London House of Graham & Co., to his son, Pierrepont, at the Union Stock Yards in Chicago. Mr. Pierrepont is worried over rumors that the old man is a bear on lard, and that the longs are about to make him climb a tree.

XVIII

Dear Pierrepont: Yours of the twenty-first inst. to hand and I note the inclosed clippings. You needn't pay any special attention to this newspaper talk about the Comstock crowd having caught me short a big line of November lard. I never sell goods without knowing where I can find them when I want them, and if these fellows try to put their forefeet in the trough, or start any shoving and crowding, they're going to find me forgetting my table manners, too. For when it comes to funny business I'm something of a humorist myself. And while I'm too old to run, I'm young enough to stand and fight.

First and last, a good many men have gone gunning for me, but they've always planned the obsequies before they caught the deceased. I reckon there hasn't been a time in twenty years when there wasn't a

259

nice " Gates Ajar " piece all made up and ready for me in some office near the Board of Trade. But the first essential of a quiet funeral is a willing corpse. And I'm still sitting up and taking nourishment.

There are two things you never want to pay any attention to—abuse and flattery. The first can't harm you and the second can't help you. Some men are like yellow dogs—when you're coming toward them they'll jump up and try to lick your hands; and when you're walking away from them they'll sneak up behind and snap at your heels. Last year, when I was bulling the market, the longs all said that I was a kind-hearted old philanthropist, who was laying awake nights scheming to get the farmers a top price for their hogs; and the shorts allowed that I was an infamous old robber, who was stealing the pork out of the workingman's pot. As long as you can't please both sides in this world, there's nothing like pleasing your own side.

There are mighty few people who can see any side to a thing except their own side. I remember once I had a vacant lot out on the Avenue, and a lady came in to my office and in a soothing-sirupy way asked if I would lend it to her, as she wanted to build a *crèche* on it. I hesitated a little, because I had never heard of a *crèche* before, and someways it sounded sort of foreign and frisky, though the woman looked like a good, safe, reliable old heifer. But she explained that a *crèche* was a baby farm, where old maids went to wash and feed and stick pins in other people's children while their mothers were off at work. Of course, there was nothing in that to get our pastor or the police after me, so I told her to go ahead.

She went off happy, but about a week later she dropped in again, looking sort of dissatisfied, to find out if I wouldn't build the

261

crèche itself. It seemed like a worthy object, so I sent some carpenters over to knock together a long frame pavilion. She was mighty grateful, you bet, and I didn't see her again for a fortnight. Then she called by to say that so long as I was in the business and they didn't cost me anything special, would I mind giving her a few cows. She had a surprised and grieved expression on her face as she talked, and the way she put it made me feel that I ought to be ashamed of myself for not having thought of the live stock myself. So I threw in half a dozen cows to provide the refreshments.

I thought that was pretty good measure, but the carpenters hadn't more than finished with the pavilion before the woman telephoned a sharp message to ask why I hadn't had it painted.

I was too busy that morning to quarrel, so I sent word that I would fix it up; and when I was driving by there next day the

painters were hard at work on it. There
was a sixty-foot frontage of that shed on the
Avenue, and I saw right off that it was just
a natural signboard. So I called over the
boss painter and between us we cooked up
a nice little ad that ran something like this:

Graham's Extract:
It Makes the Weak Strong.

Well, sir, when she saw the ad next morning that old hen just scratched gravel.
Went all around town saying that I had
given a five-hundred-dollar shed to charity
and painted a thousand-dollar ad on it. Allowed I ought to send my check for that
amount to the *crèche* fund. Kept at it till
I began to think there might be something
in it, after all, and sent her the money.
Then I found a fellow who wanted to build
in that neighborhood, sold him the lot cheap,
and got out of the *crèche* industry.

I've put a good deal more than work into
my business, and I've drawn a good deal

more than money out of it; but the only
thing I've ever put into it which didn't draw
dividends in fun or dollars was worry.
That is a branch of the trade which you
want to leave to our competitors.

I've always found worrying a blamed
sight more uncertain than horse-racing—
it's harder to pick a winner at it. You go
home worrying because you're afraid that
your fool new clerk forgot to lock the safe
after you, and during the night the lard
refinery burns down; you spend a year
fretting because you think Bill Jones is
going to cut you out with your best girl, and
then you spend ten worrying because he
didn't; you worry over Charlie at college
because he's a little wild, and he writes you
that he's been elected president of the Y.
M. C. A.; and you worry over William because he's so pious that you're afraid he's
going to throw up everything and go to
China as a missionary, and he draws on you
for a hundred; you worry because you're

afraid your business is going to smash, and your health busts up instead. Worrying is the one game in which, if you guess right, you don't get any satisfaction out of your smartness. A busy man has no time to bother with it. He can always find plenty of old women in skirts or trousers to spend their days worrying over their own troubles and to sit up nights waking his.

Speaking of handing over your worries to others naturally calls to mind the Widow Williams and her son Bud, who was a playmate of mine when I was a boy. Bud was the youngest of the Widow's troubles, and she was a woman whose troubles seldom came singly. Had fourteen altogether, and four pair of 'em were twins. Used to turn 'em loose in the morning, when she let out her cows and pigs to browse along the street, and then she'd shed all worry over them for the rest of the day. Allowed that if they got hurt the neighbors would bring them home; and that if they got hungry they'd come home. And someways, the whole drove always showed up safe and dirty about meal time.

I've no doubt she thought a lot of Bud, but when a woman has fourteen it sort of unsettles her mind so that she can't focus her affections or play any favorites. And so when Bud's clothes were found at the swimming hole one day, and no Bud inside them, she didn't take on up to the expectations of the neighbors who had brought the news, and who were standing around waiting for her to go off into something special in the way of high-strikes.

She allowed that they were Bud's clothes, all right, but she wanted to know where the remains were. Hinted that there'd be no funeral, or such like expensive goings-on, until some one produced the deceased. Take her by and large, she was a pretty cool, calm cucumber.

But if she showed a little too much Christian resignation, the rest of the town was mightily stirred up over Bud's death, and every one just quit work to tell each other what a noble little fellow he was; and how his mother hadn't deserved to have such a bright little sunbeam in her home; and to drag the river between talks. But they couldn't get a rise.

Through all the worry and excitement the Widow was the only one who didn't show any special interest, except to ask for results. But finally, at the end of a week, when they'd strained the whole river through their drags and hadn't anything to show for it but a collection of tin cans and dead catfish, she threw a shawl over her head and went down the street to the cabin of Louisiana Clytemnestra, an old yellow woman, who would go into a trance for four bits and find a fortune for you for a dollar. I reckon she'd have called herself a clairvoyant nowadays, but then she was just a voodoo woman.

Well, the Widow said she reckoned that

boys ought to be let out as well as in for half price, and so she laid down two bits, allowing that she wanted a few minutes' private conversation with her Bud. Clytie said she'd do her best, but that spirits were mighty snifty and high-toned, even when they'd only been poor white trash on earth, and it might make them mad to be called away from their high jinks if they were taking a little recreation, or from their high-priced New York customers if they were working, to tend to cut-rate business. Still, she'd have a try, and she did. But after having convulsions for half an hour, she gave it up. Reckoned that Bud was up to some cussedness off somewhere, and that he wouldn't answer for any two-bits.

The Widow was badly disappointed, but she allowed that that was just like Bud. He'd always been a boy that never could be found when any one wanted him. So she went off, saying that she'd had her money's worth in seeing Clytie throw those fancy

*" Elder Hoover was accounted a
powerful exhorter in our parts."*

fits. But next day she came again and paid
down four bits, and Clytie reckoned that
that ought to fetch Bud sure. Someways
though, she didn't have any luck, and finally
the Widow suggested that she call up Bud's
father—Buck Williams had been dead a
matter of ten years—and the old man re-
sponded promptly.

"Where's Bud?" asked the Widow.

Hadn't laid eyes on him. Didn't know
he'd come across. Had he joined the church
before he started?

"No."

Then he'd have to look downstairs for
him.

Clytie told the Widow to call again and
they'd get him sure. So she came back next
day and laid down a dollar. That fetched
old Buck Williams' ghost on the jump, you
bet, but he said he hadn't laid eyes on Bud
yet. They hauled the Sweet By and By with
a drag net, but they couldn't get a rap from
him. Clytie trotted out George Washing-

ton, and Napoleon, and Billy Patterson, and Ben Franklin, and Captain Kidd, just to show that there was no deception, but they couldn't get a whisper even from Bud.

I reckon Clytie had been stringing the old lady along, intending to produce Bud's spook as a sort of red-fire, calcium-light, grand-march-of-the-Amazons climax, but she didn't get a chance. For right there the old lady got up with a mighty set expression around her lips and marched out, muttering that it was just as she had thought all along —Bud wasn't there. And when the neighbors dropped in that afternoon to plan out a memorial service for her " lost lamb," she chased them off the lot with a broom. Said that they had looked in the river for him and that she had looked beyond the river for him, and that they would just stand pat now and wait for him to make the next move. Allowed that if she could once get her hands in " that lost lamb's " wool there might be an opening for a funeral when she got through with him, but there wouldn't be till then. Altogether, it looked as if there was a heap of trouble coming to Bud if he had made any mistake and was still alive.

The Widow found her " lost lamb " hiding behind a rain-barrel when she opened up the house next morning, and there was a mighty touching and affecting scene. In fact, the Widow must have touched him at least a hundred times and every time he was affected to tears, for she was using a bed slat, which is a powerfully strong moral agent for making a boy see the error of his ways. And it was a month after that before Bud could go down Main Street without some man who had called him a noble little fellow, or a bright, manly little chap, while he was drowned, reaching out and fetching him a clip on the ear for having come back and put the laugh on him.

No one except the Widow ever really got at the straight of Bud's conduct, but it appeared that he left home to get a few Indian scalps, and that he came back for a little bacon and corn pone.

I simply mention the Widow in passing as an example of the fact that the time to do your worrying is when a thing is all over, and that the way to do it is to leave it to the neighbors. I sail for home to-morrow.

Your affectionate father,
JOHN GRAHAM.

No. 19

FROM John Graham, at the New York house of Graham & Co., to his son, Pierrepont, at the Union Stock Yards in Chicago. The old man, on the voyage home, has met a girl who interests him and who in turn seems to be interested in Mr. Pierrepont.

XIX

Dear Pierrepont: Who is this Helen
Heath, and what are your intentions there?
She knows a heap more about you than she
ought to know if they're not serious, and I
know a heap less about her than I ought to
know if they are. Hadn't got out of sight of
land before we'd become acquainted somehow, and she's been treating me like a father
clear across the Atlantic. She's a mighty
pretty girl, and a mighty nice girl, and a
mighty sensible girl—in fact she's so exactly
the sort of girl I'd like to see you marry that
I'm afraid there's nothing in it.

Of course, your salary isn't a large one
yet, but you can buy a whole lot of happiness
with fifty dollars a week when you have the
right sort of a woman for your purchasing
agent. And while I don't go much on love
in a cottage, love in a flat, with fifty a week
as a starter, is just about right, if the girl is

275

just about right. If she isn't, it doesn't make any special difference how you start out, you're going to end up all wrong.

Money ought never to be *the* consideration in marriage, but it always ought to be *a* consideration. When a boy and a girl don't think enough about money before the ceremony, they're going to have to think altogether too much about it after; and when a man's doing sums at home evenings, it comes kind of awkward for him to try to hold his wife on his lap.

There's nothing in this talk that two can live cheaper than one. A good wife doubles a man's expenses and doubles his happiness, and that's a pretty good investment if a fellow's got the money to invest. I have met women who had cut their husband's expenses in half, but they needed the money because they had doubled their own. I might add, too, that I've met a good many husbands who had cut their wives' expenses in half, and they fit naturally into any dis-

276

cussion of our business, because they are hogs. There's a point where economy becomes a vice, and that's when a man leaves its practice to his wife.

An unmarried man is a good deal like a piece of unimproved real estate—he may be worth a whole lot of money, but he isn't of any particular use except to build on. The great trouble with a lot of these fellows is that they're "made land," and if you dig down a few feet you strike ooze and booze under the layer of dollars that their daddies dumped in on top. Of course, the only way to deal with a proposition of that sort is to drive forty-foot piles clear down to solid rock and then to lay railroad iron and cement till you've got something to build on. But a lot of women will go right ahead without any preliminaries and wonder what's the matter when the walls begin to crack and tumble about their ears.

I never come across a case of this sort without thinking of Jack Carter, whose father died about ten years ago and left Jack a million dollars, and left me as trustee of both until Jack reached his twenty-fifth birthday. I didn't relish the job particularly, because Jack was one of these charlotte-russe boys, all whipped cream and sponge cake and high-priced flavoring extracts, without any filling qualities. There wasn't any special harm in him, but there wasn't any special good, either, and I always feel that there's more hope for a fellow who's an out and out cuss than for one who's simply made up of a lot of little trifling meannesses. Jack wore mighty warm clothes and mighty hot vests, and the girls all said that he was a perfect dream, but I've never been one who could get a great deal of satisfaction out of dreams.

It's mighty seldom that I do an exhibition mile, but the winter after I inherited Jack —he was twenty-three years old then—your Ma kept after me so strong that I finally put on my fancy harness and let her trot me

around to a meet at the Ralstons one evening. Of course, I was in the Percheron
class, and so I just stood around with a lot
of heavy old draft horses, who ought to have
been resting up in their stalls, and watched
the three-year-olds prance and cavort round
the ring. Jack was among them, of course,
dancing with the youngest Churchill girl,
and holding her a little tighter, I thought,
than was necessary to keep her from falling.
Had both ends working at once—never
missed a stitch with his heels and was turning out a steady stream of fancy work with
his mouth. And all the time he was looking at that girl as intent and eager as a
Scotch terrier at a rat hole.

I happened just then to be pinned into a
corner with two or three women who
couldn't escape—Edith Curzon, a great big
brunette whom I knew Jack had been pretty
soft on, and little Mabel Moore, a nice roly-
poly blonde, and it didn't take me long to
see that they were watching Jack with a

hair-pulling itch in their finger-tips. In fact, it looked to me as if the young scamp was a good deal more popular than the facts about him, as I knew them, warranted him in being.

I slipped out early, but next evening, when I was sitting in my little smoking-room, Jack came charging in, and, without any sparring for an opening, burst out with:

" Isn't she a stunner, Mr. Graham ! "

I allowed that Miss Curzon was something on the stun.

" Miss Curzon, indeed," he sniffed. " She's well enough in a big, black way, but Miss Churchill——" and he began to paw the air for adjectives.

" But how was I to know that you meant Miss Churchill? " I answered. " It's just a fortnight now since you told me that Miss Curzon was a goddess, and that she was going to reign in your life and make it a heaven, or something of that sort. I forget just the words, but they were mighty beautiful thoughts and did you credit."

"Don't remind me of it," Jack groaned. "It makes me sick every time I think what an ass I've been."

I allowed that I felt a little nausea myself, but I told him that this time, at least, he'd shown some sense; that Miss Churchill was a mighty pretty girl and rich enough so that her liking him didn't prove anything worse against her than bad judgment; and that the thing for him to do was to quit his foolishness, propose to her, and dance the heel, toe, and a one, two, three with her for the rest of his natural days.

Jack hemmed and hawked a little over this, but finally he came out with it:

"That's the deuce of it," says he. "I'm in a beastly mess—I want to marry her— she's the only girl in the world for me—the only one I've ever really loved, and I've proposed—that is, I want to propose to her, but I'm engaged to Edith Curzon on the quiet."

" I reckon you'll marry her, then," I said; " because she strikes me as a young woman who's not going to lose a million dollars without putting a tracer after it."

" And that's not the worst of it," Jack went on.

" Not the worst of it! What do you mean! You haven't married her on the quiet, too, have you? "

" No, but there's Mabel Moore, you know."

I didn't know, but I guessed. " You haven't been such a double-barreled donkey as to give her an option on yourself, too? "

" No, no; but I've said things to her which she may have misconstrued, if she's inclined to be literal."

" You bet she is," I answered. " I never saw a nice, fat, blonde girl who took a million-dollar offer as a practical joke. What is it you've said to her? ' I love you, darling,' or something about as foxy and non-committal."

" Not that—not that at all; but she may have stretched what I said to mean that."

Well, sir, I just laid into that fellow when I heard that, though I could see that he didn't think it was refined of me. He'd never made it any secret that he thought me a pretty coarse old man, and his face showed me now that I was jarring his delicate works.

" I suppose I have been indiscreet," he said, " but I must say I expected something different from you, after coming out this way and owning up. Of course, if you don't care to help me——"

I cut him short there. " I've got to help you. But I want you to tell me the truth. How have you managed to keep this Curzon girl from announcing her engagement to you? "

" Well," and there was a scared grin on

283

Jack's face now; " I told her that you, as trustee under father's will, had certain unpleasant powers over my money—in fact, that most of it would revert to Sis if I married against your wishes, and that you disliked her, and that she must work herself into your good graces before we could think of announcing our engagement."

I saw right off that he had told Mabel Moore the same thing, and that was why those two girls had been so blamed polite to me the night before. So I rounded on him sudden.

" You're engaged to that Miss Moore, too, aren't you? "

" I'm afraid so."

" Why didn't you come out like a man and say so at first? "

" I couldn't, Mr. Graham. Someways it seemed like piling it up so, and you take such a cold-blooded, unsympathetic view of these things."

284

" Perhaps I do; yes, I'm afraid I do. How far are you committed to Miss Churchill? "

Jack cheered right up. " I'm all right there, at least. She hasn't answered."

" Then you've asked? "

" Why, so I have; at least she may take it for something like asking. But I don't care; I want to be committed there; I can't live without her; she's the only——"

I saw that he was beginning to foam up again, so I shut him off straight at the spigot. Told him to save it till after the ceremony. Set him down to my desk, and dictated two letters, one to Edith Curzon and the other to Mabel Moore, and made him sign and seal them, then and there. He twisted and squirmed and tried to wiggle off the hook, but I wouldn't give him any slack. Made him come right out and say that he was a yellow pup; that he had made a mistake; and that the stuff was all off, though I worded it a little different from that. Slung in some fancy words and high-toned phrases.

You see, I had made up my mind that the best of a bad matter was the Churchill girl, and I didn't propose to have her commit herself, too, until I'd sort of cleared away the wreckage. Then I reckoned on copper-riveting their engagement by announcing it myself and standing over Jack with a shot-gun to see that there wasn't any more non-sense. They were both so light-headed and light-waisted and light-footed that it seemed to me that they were just naturally mates.

Jack reached for those letters when they were addressed and started to put them in his pocket, but I had reached first. I reckon he'd decided that something might happen to them on their way to the post-office; but nothing did, for I called in the butler and made him go right out and mail them then and there.

I'd had the letters dated from my house, and I made Jack spend the night there. I reckoned it might be as well to keep him within reaching distance for the next day or two. He showed up at breakfast in the morning looking like a calf on the way to the killing pens, and I could see that his thoughts were mighty busy following the postman who was delivering those letters. I tried to cheer him up by reading some little odds and ends from the morning paper about other people's troubles, but they didn't seem to interest him.

"They must just about have received them," he finally groaned into his coffee cup. "Why did I send them! What will those girls think of me! They'll cut me dead— never speak to me again."

The butler came in before I could tell him that this was about what we'd calculated on their doing, and said: "Beg pardon, sir, but there's a lady asking for you at the telephone."

"A lady!" says Jack. "Tell her I'm not here." Talk to one of those girls, even from

287

a safe distance! He guessed not. He turned as pale as a hog on ice at the thought of it.

"I'm sorry, sir," said the man, "but I've already said that you were breakfasting here. She said it was very important."

I could see that Jack's curiosity was already getting the best of his scare. After all, he threw out, feeling me, it might be best to hear what she had to say. I thought so, too, and he went to the instrument and shouted "Hello!" in what he tried to make a big, brave voice, but it wobbled a little all the same.

I got the other end of the conversation from him when he was through.

"Hello! Is that you, Jack?" chirped the Curzon girl.

"Yes. Who is that?"

"Edith," came back. "I have your letter, but I can't make out what it's all about. Come this afternoon and tell me, for we're still good friends, aren't we, Jack?"

"Yes—certainly," stammered Jack.

" And you'll come? "

" Yes," he answered, and cut her off.

He had hardly recovered from this shock when a messenger boy came with a note, addressed in a woman's writing.

" Now for it," he said, and breaking the seal read :

" ' *Jack dear:* Your horrid note doesn't say anything, nor explain anything. Come this afternoon and tell what it means to

M<small>ABEL</small>.' "

" Here's a go," exclaimed Jack, but he looked pleased in a sort of sneaking way. " What do you think of it, Mr. Graham? "

" I don't like it."

" Think they intend to cut up? " he asked.

" Like a sausage machine; and yet I don't see how they can stand for you after that letter."

" Well, shall I go? "

" Yes, in fact I suppose you must go; but Jack, be a man. Tell 'em plain and straight that you don't love 'em as you should to marry 'em; say you saw your old girl a few days ago and found you loved her still, or something from the same trough, and stick to it. Take what you deserve. If they hold you up to the bull-ring, the only thing you can do is to propose to take the whole bunch to Utah, and let 'em share and share alike. That'll settle it. Be firm."

" As a rock, sir."

I made Jack come downtown and lunch with me, but when I started him off, about two o'clock, he looked so like a cat padding up the back-stairs to where she knows there's a little canary meat—scared, but happy—that I said once more: " Now be firm, Jack."

" Firm's the word, sir," was the resolute answer.

" And unyielding."

" As the old guard." And Jack puffed himself out till he was as chesty as a pigeon on a barn roof, and swung off down the street looking mighty fine and manly from the rear.

I never really got the straight of it, but I pieced together these particulars later. At the corner there was a flower store. Jack stepped inside and sent a box of roses by special messenger to Miss Curzon, so there might be something to start conversation when he got there. Two blocks farther on he passed a second florist's, turned back and sent some lilies to Miss Moore, for fear she might think he'd forgotten her during the hour or more before he could work around to her house. Then he chased about and found a third florist, from whom he ordered some violets for Miss Churchill, to remind her that she had promised him the first dance at the Blairs' that night. Your Ma told me that Jack had nice instincts about these little things which women like, and always put a good deal of heavy thought into selecting his flowers for them. It's been my experience that a critter who has instincts instead of sense belongs in the bushes with the dicky-birds.

No one ever knew just what happened to Jack during the next three hours. He showed up at his club about five o'clock with a mighty conceited set to his jaw, but it dropped as if the spring had broken when he caught sight of me waiting for him in the reading-room.

" You here? " he asked as he threw himself into a chair.

" You bet," I said. " I wanted to hear how you made out. You settled the whole business, I take it? " but I knew mighty well from his looks that he hadn't settled anything.

" Not—not exactly—that is to say, entirely; but I've made a very satisfactory beginning."

" Began it all over again, I suppose."

This hit so near the truth that Jack jumped, in spite of himself, and then he burst out with a really swear. I couldn't have been more surprised if your Ma had cussed.

"Damn it, sir, I won't stand any more of your confounded meddling. Those letters were a piece of outrageous brutality. I'm breaking off with the girls, but I've gone about it in a gentler and, I hope, more dignified, way."

"Jack, I don't believe any such stuff and guff. You're tied up to them harder and tighter than ever."

I could see I'd made a bull's eye, for Jack began to bluster, but I cut him short with:

"Go to the devil your own way," and walked out of the club. I reckon that Jack felt mighty disturbed for as much as an hour, but a good dinner took the creases out of his system. He'd found that Miss Moore didn't intend to go to the Blairs', and that Miss Curzon had planned to go to a dance with her sister somewheres else, so he calculated on having a clear track for a trial spin with Miss Churchill.

I surprised your Ma a good deal that evening by allowing that I'd go to the Blairs' myself, for it looked to me as if the finals might be trotted there, and I thought I'd better be around, because, while I didn't see much chance of getting any sense into Jack's head, I felt I ought to do what I could on my friendship account with his father.

Jack was talking to Miss Churchill when I came into the room, and he was tending to business so strictly that he didn't see me bearing down on him from one side of the room, nor Edith Curzon's sister, Mrs. Dick, a mighty capable young married woman, bearing down on him from the other, nor Miss Curzon, with one of his roses in her hair, watching him from a corner. There must have been a council of war between the sisters that afternoon, and a change of their plans for the evening.

Mrs. Dick beat me stalking Jack, but I was just behind, a close second. He didn't

" *Miss Curzon, with one of
his roses in her hair, watching
him from a corner.*"

see her until she got right up to him and rapped him on the arm with her fan.

" Dear Jack," she says, all smiles and sugar; " dear Jack, I've just heard. Edith has told me, though I'd suspected something for a long, long time, you rogue," and she fetched him another kittenish clip with the fan.

Jack looked about the way I once saw old Miss Curley, the president of the Good Templars back in our town in Missouri, look at a party when she half-swallowed a spoonful of her ice cream before she discovered that it was flavored with liquor.

But he stammered something and hurried Miss Churchill away, though not before a fellow who was going by had wrung his hand and said, " Congratulations, old chap. Just heard the news."

Jack's only idea seemed to travel, and to travel far and fast, and he dragged his partner along to the other end of the room, while

I followed the band. We had almost gone the length of the course, when Jack, who had been staring ahead mighty hard, shied and balked, for there, not ten feet away, stood Miss Moore, carrying his lilies, and blushing and smiling at something young Blakely was saying to her.

I reckon Jack guessed what that something was, but just then Blakely caught sight of him and rushed up to where he was standing.

"I congratulate you, Jack," he said. "Miss Moore's a charming girl."

And now Miss Churchill slipped her hand from his arm and turned and looked at Jack. Her lips were laughing, but there was something in her eye which made Jack turn his own away.

"Oh, you lucky Jack," she laughed. "You twice lucky Jack."

Jack simply curled up: "Wretched mistake somewhere," he mumbled. "Awfully hot here—get you a glass of water," and he

296

rushed off. He dodged around Miss Moore, and made a flank movement which got him by Miss Curzon and safely to the door. He kept on; I followed.

I had to go to New York on business next day. Jack had already gone there, bought a ticket for Europe, and was just loafing around the pier trying to hurry the steamer off. I went down to see him start, and he looked so miserable that I'd have felt sorry for him if I hadn't seen him look miserable before.

"Is it generally known, sir, do you think?" he asked me humbly. "Can't you hush it up somehow?"

"Hush it up! You might as well say 'Shoo!' to the Limited and expect it to stop for you."

"Mr. Graham, I'm simply heartbroken over it all. I know I shall never reach Liverpool. I'll go mad on the voyage across, and throw myself overboard. I'm too delicately strung to stand a thing of this sort."

"Delicate rats! You haven't nerve enough not to stand it," I said. "Brace up and be a man, and let this be a lesson to you. Good-bye."

Jack took my hand sort of mechanically and looked at me without seeing me, for his grief-dimmed eyes, in straying along the deck, had lit on that pretty little Southern baggage, Fanny Fairfax. And as I started off he was leaning over her in the same old way, looking into her brown eyes as if he saw a full-course dinner there.

"Think of *your* being on board!" I heard him say. "I'm the luckiest fellow alive; by Jove, I am!"

I gave Jack up, and an ex-grass widow is keeping him in order now. I don't go much on grass widows, but I give her credit for doing a pretty good job. She's got Jack so tame that he eats out of her hand, and so well trained that he don't allow strangers to pet him.

I inherited one Jack—I couldn't help

that. But I don't propose to wake up and find another one in the family. So you write me what's what by return.

Your affectionate father,

JOHN GRAHAM.

No. 20

FROM John Graham, at the Boston House of Graham & Co., to his son, Pierrepont, at the Union Stock Yards in Chicago. Mr. Pierrepont has told the old man "what's what" and received a limited blessing.

XX

Dear Pierrepont: If that's what, it's all right. And you can't get married too quick to suit the old man. I believe in short engagements and long marriages. I don't see any sense in a fellow's sitting around on the mourner's bench with the sinners, after he's really got religion. The time to size up the other side's strength is before the engagement.

Some fellows propose to a girl before they know whether her front and her back hair match, and then holler that they're stuck when they find that she's got a cork leg and a glass eye as well. I haven't any sympathy with them. They start out on the principle that married people have only one meal a day, and that of fried oysters and tutti-frutti ice-cream after the theatre. Naturally, a girl's got her better nature and her best complexion along under those circum-

303

stances; but the really valuable thing to know is how she approaches ham and eggs at seven A. M., and whether she brings her complexion with her to the breakfast table. And these fellows make a girl believe that they're going to spend all the time between eight and eleven P. M., for the rest of their lives, holding a hundred and forty pounds, live weight, in their lap, and saying that it feels like a feather. The thing to find out is whether, when one of them gets up to holding a ten pound baby in his arms, for five minutes, he's going to carry on as if it weighed a ton.

A girl can usually catch a whisper to the effect that she's the showiest goods on the shelf, but the vital thing for a fellow to know is whether her ears are sharp enough to hear him when he shouts that she's spending too much money and that she must reduce expenses. Of course, when you're patting and petting and feeding a woman she's going to purr, but there's nothing like stirring her

up a little now and then to see if she spits
fire and heaves things when she's mad.

I want to say right here that there's only
one thing more aggravating in this world
than a woman who gets noisy when she's
mad, and that's one who gets quiet. The
first breaks her spell of temper with the
crockery, but the second simmers along
like a freight engine on the track beside
your berth—keeps you scared and ready to
jump for fear she's going to blow off any
minute; but she never does and gets it over
with—just drizzles it out.

You can punch your brother when he
plays the martyr, but you've got to love your
wife. A violent woman drives a fellow to
drink, but a nagging one drives him crazy.
She takes his faults and ties them to him
like a tin can to a yellow dog's tail, and the
harder he runs to get away from them the
more he hears of them.

I simply mention these things in a general
way, and in the spirit of the preacher at the

funeral of the man who wasn't "a professor"—because it's customary to make a few
appropriate remarks on these occasions.
From what I saw of Helen Heath, I reckon
she's not getting any the best of it. She's
what I call a mighty eligible young woman—
pretty, bright, sensible, and without any
fortune to make her foolish and you a fool.
In fact, you'd have to sit up nights to make
yourself good enough for her, even if you
brought her a million, instead of fifty a
week.

I'm a great believer in women in the home,
but I don't take much stock in them in the
office, though I reckon I'm prejudiced and
they've come to stay. I never do business
with a woman that I don't think of a little
incident which happened when I was first
married to your Ma. We set up housekeeping in one of those cottages that you read
about in the story books, but that you want
to shy away from, when it's put up to you to
live in one of them. There were nice climb-

ing roses on the front porch, but no running water in the kitchen; there were a-plenty of old fashioned posies in the front yard, and a-plenty of rats in the cellar; there was half an acre of ground out back, but so little room inside that I had to sit with my feet out a window. It was just the place to go for a picnic, but it's been my experience that a fellow does most of his picnicking before he's married.

Your Ma did the cooking, and I hustled for things to cook, though I would take a shy at it myself once in a while and get up my muscle tossing flapjacks. It was pretty rough sailing, you bet, but one way and another we managed to get a good deal of satisfaction out of it, because we had made up our minds to take our fun as we went along. With most people happiness is something that is always just a day off. But I have made it a rule never to put off being happy till to-morrow. Don't accept notes for happiness, because you'll find that when they're due they're never paid, but just renewed for another thirty days.

I was clerking in a general store at that time, but I had a little weakness for live-stock, even then; and while I couldn't af-ford to plunge in it exactly, I managed to buy a likely little shoat that I reckoned on carrying through the Summer on credit and presenting with a bill for board in the Fall. He was just a plain pig when he came to us, and we kept him in a little sty, but we weren't long in finding out that he wasn't any ordinary root-and-grunt pig. The first I knew your Ma was calling him Toby, and had turned him loose. Answered to his name like a dog. Never saw such a sociable pig. Wanted to sit on the porch with us. Tried to come into the house evenings. Used to run down the road squealing for joy when he saw me coming home from work.

Well, it got on towards November and Toby had been making the most of his op-portunities. I never saw a pig that turned corn into fat so fast, and the stouter he got the better his disposition grew. I reckon I was attached to him myself, in a sort of a sneaking way, but I was mighty fond of hog meat, too, and we needed Toby in the kitchen. So I sent around and had him butchered.

When I got home to dinner next day, I noticed that your Ma looked mighty solemn as she set the roast of pork down in front of me, but I strayed off, thinking of something else, as I carved, and my wits were off wool gathering sure enough when I said:

"Will you have a piece of Toby, my dear?"

Well sir, she just looked at me for a moment, and then she burst out crying and ran away from the table. But when I went after her and asked her what was the matter, she stopped crying and was mad in a minute all the way through. Called me a heartless, cruel cannibal. That seemed to relieve her so that she got over her mad

and began to cry again. Begged me to take
Toby out of pickle and to bury him in the
garden. I reasoned with her, and in the end
I made her see that any obsequies for Toby,
with pork at eight cents a pound, would be a
pretty expensive funeral for us. But first
and last she had managed to take my appetite away so that I didn't want any roast
pork for dinner or cold pork for supper.
That night I took what was left of Toby
to a store keeper at the Crossing, who I
knew would be able to gaze on his hams
without bursting into tears, and got a pretty
fair price for him.

I simply mention Toby in passing, as an
example of why I believe women weren't
cut out for business—at least for the pork-
packing business. I've had dealings with a
good many of them, first and last, and it's
been my experience that when they've got a
weak case they add their sex to it and win,
and that when they've got a strong case they
subtract their sex from it and deal with you

harder than a man. They're simply bound to win either way, and I don't like to play a game where I haven't any show. When a clerk makes a fool break, I don't want to beg his pardon for calling his attention to it, and I don't want him to blush and tremble and leak a little brine into a fancy pocket handkerchief.

A little change is a mighty soothing thing, and I like a woman's ways too much at home to care very much for them at the office. Instead of hiring women, I try to hire their husbands, and then I usually have them both working for me. There's nothing like a woman at home to spur on a man at the office.

A married man is worth more salary than a single one, because his wife makes him worth more. He's apt to go to bed a little sooner and to get up a little earlier; to go a little steadier and to work a little harder than the fellow who's got to amuse a different girl every night, and can't stay at home to do it. That's why I'm going to raise your salary to seventy-five dollars a week the day you marry Helen, and that's why I'm going to quit writing these letters—I'm simply going to turn you over to her and let her keep you in order. I bet she'll do a better job than I have.

Your affectionate father,

JOHN GRAHAM.

THE END